INDIAN WILDLIFE QUIZ

INDIAN WILDLIFE QUIZ

Deep Narayan Pandey

RUPA

Published by
Rupa Publications India Pvt. Ltd 2004
7/16, Ansari Road, Daryaganj
New Delhi 110002

Sales Centres:

Allahabad Bengaluru Chennai
Hyderabad Jaipur Kathmandu
Kolkata Mumbai

ISBN: 978-81-716-7045-1

Fifth impression 2016

10 9 8 7 6 5

ACKNOWLEDGEMENTS

I am grateful to several of my colleagues including Samir Dubey, Shashi Paul, Rajiv Gupta, Dhananjai Mohan, R. K. Mishra and Deep Shekhar for advice and comments. I am particularly indebted to Prof. S. C. Sinha, Rajesh Gopal and S. L. Wadhera for helping me in various ways.

I wish to express my appreciation for the cooperation and institutional help I received from J. B. Lal, Director General, Indian Council for Forestry Research and Education, Dehra Dun; S. K. Pande, Director, Indira Gandhi National Forest Academy, Dehra Dun, and B. N. Yugandhar, Director, Lal Bahadur Shastri National Academy of Administration, Mussoorie.

I am thankful to Kailash Sankhala and V. D. Sharma for valuable suggestions and encouragement. I have drawn heavily on the resources of Sundeep Nayak, A. J. T. Johnsingh, V. B. Sawarkar, H. S. Panwar, Fateh Singh Rathor, Valmik Thapar, Bharat Taimni, N. Uday Shekar, Dhananjai Mohan, Abhijit Ghosh and Dr S. S. Negi. I am indebted to them all.

It is with pleasure that I acknowledge the guidance I received from S. Dillon Ripley, Secretary Emeritus of the Smithsonian Institution, Washington D.C., and H. S. Panwar, Director, Wildlife Institute of India, Dehra Dun.

Thanks are also due to Ms Manjula and Ms Prem for painstaking assistance in typing and preparation of the draft.

PREFACE

Depletion, endangerment and extinction are not just high-sounding phrases but naked realities today. Over-exploitation, habitat destruction and our own ignorance and inability about the impending disaster, are largely responsible for the environmental crisis.

Our pursuit of profit and development seems to have been trotting on a wrong path. Global environmental mismanagement has shown enough evidence to warn us about playing with glowing fire. It is high time that we explain and satisfy ourselves that nature conservation is the most important factor for socio-economic development of mankind; and more relevant, it ensures our survival. If environment is protected, we would continue to harvest clean water, fresh air and sweet fruits of nature with ensured sustainability of life support systems.

It is to remind fellow citizens of our planet the *Indian Wildlife Quiz* presents facts for analysis and action. The book presents rich biodiversity and beauty of Indian wilderness. The first eleven chapters are devoted to various facets of conservation of Indian flora, fauna and habitat and the last chapter gives an insight into the wild genetic resource and contemporary world wildlife conservation.

I sincerely hope the book will prove its worth in generating interest and in eliminating the environmental illiteracy and carry the message that without conservation of all life forms and without protecting environment, human race cannot sustain for long.

Deep Narayan Pandey

CONTENTS

1

GLIMPSES OF INDIAN
NATURAL HISTORY

1. Which National Park in India is famous as the wintering ground for the Siberian Crane (*Grus leucogeranus*)?
   (a) Keoladeo, Rajasthan (b) Dudhwa, U.P. (c) Kanha, M.P. (d) Bandhavgarh, M.P.

2. Who painted 'Tiger Fire' to raise funds for Operation Tiger?
   (a) David Shepherd (b) Zai Whitaker (c) Jim Corbett (d) David Lock

3. Name the only Indian recipient of the prestigious Paul Getty Award for conservation:
   (a) S. Dillon Ripley (b) Dr. Salim Ali (b) Bharat Bhusan (d) Zafer Futehally

4. Name the only Indian state where all three species of the Indian Crocodile—Gharial, Muggar, Saltwater Crocodile—are found in the wild:
   (a) M.P. (b) U.P. (c) Orissa (d) West Bengal

5. Which is the longest of all snakes in the world?
   (a) Indian Python (*Python molurus*) (b) Reticulated Python (*Python reticulatus*) (c) King Cobra (*Ophiophagus hannah*) (d) Indian Cobra (*Naja naja*)

6. Give the popular name of the convention on conservation of migratory wild animals:
   (a) Bonn Convention (b) Ramsar Convention (c) Corbett Declaration (d) Delhi Declaration

7. Name a protected area (Reserve) in India which has been created in the name of a primitive tribe to protect and safeguard the culture of these people:

    (a) Kanger National Park, MP (b) Nokrek (c) Jarwa Tribal Reserve, Middle Andaman (d) None of the above

8. Name the National Park that holds the only viable population of wild buffalo in Central India. It is also a possible alternative home for the swamp deer of Kanha National Park:

    (a) Satpura National Park (b) Tadoba National Park (c) Kanha National Park (d) Indravati N.P. and Tiger Reserve

9. Which is the 18th Tiger Reserve of India to be created under the 'Project Tiger'?

    (a) Kalakad Mundanthurai (b) Dudhwa (c) Buxa (d) Valmiki

10. Name the smallest true deer of the Indian sub-continent:

    (a) Hog Deer (*Axis porcinus*) (b) Muntjak (*Muntiacus muntjak*) (c) Indian chevrotain (*Tragulus meminna*)   (d) Chital (*Axis axis*)

11. Which bird in India has the longest legs?

    (a) Common Crane (*Grus grus*) (b) Saras Crane (*Grus antigone*) (c) Siberian Crane (*Grus leucogeranus*) (d) Demoiselle crane (*Anthropoides virgo*)

12. There is a bamboo in India that produces very large fleshy fruits, of the size of guavas—people collect these fruits for food. Name this bamboo:

    (a) *Dondrocalamus strictus* (b) *Melocana bambusoides* (c) *Melocana baccifera* (d) *Bambusa vulgaris*

13. Which national park or sanctuary in India is popularly known as Floating National Park? It is meant to protect a rare species of Indian deer.
(a) Keibul Lamjao National Park (b) Chilka Sanctuary (c) Jaisamand Sanctuary (d) Keoladeo Ghana National Park

14. Name the only wild goat found in the peninsular India (South India):
(a) Wild goat (*Capra hircus*) (b) Markhor (*Capra falconeri*) (c) Nilgiri Tahr (*Hemitragus hylocrius*) (d) Goral (*Nemorhaedus goral*)

15. What is the young one (new-born) of the whale called?
(a) Calf (b) Baby (c) Cub (d) Pup

16. Name the bird, the incidental shooting of which created circumstances for Salim Ali to become a world famous ornithologist:
(a) House sparrow (*Passer domesticus*) (b) Tree sparrow (*Passer montanus*) (c) Scrub sparrow (*Passer moabiticus*) (d) Yellow throated sparrow (*Petronia xanthocollis*)

17. Name the smallest wild cat in India:
(a) Pallas's cat (*Felis manul*) (b) Rustyspotted cat (*Felis rubiginosa*) (c) Fishing Cat (*Felis viverrina*) (d) Golden cat (*Felis temmincki*)

18. Name the bird which was found only in Mussoorie and Nainital areas of Western Himalaya and now is considered extinct:
(a) Bamboo Partridge (*Bambusicola fytchii*) (b) Mountain Quail (*Ophrysia superciliosa*) (c) Jungle Bush Quail (*Perdicula asiatica*) (d) Button Quail (*Turnix tanki*)

19. Which biogeographic zone sustains the largest number of endangered species?
    (a) North-East (b) Central India (c) Islands (d) Coasts

20. Where is the headquarters of the Wildlife Preservation Society of India situated?
    (a) Dehra Dun (b) Mussoorie (c) Guwahati (d) Bombay

21. Which frog is the prettiest of all living Indian amphibians based on the colour pattern of the body?
    (a) Indian Bull Frog (*Rana tigrina*) (b) Ceylone Kaloula (*Kaloula pulchra taprobanica*) (c) Variable Ramanella (*Ramanella variegata*) (d) None

22. Which noted Indian conservationist is popularly known as Billy?
    (a) Salim Ali (b) Romulus Whitaker (c) Arjan Singh (d) Kailash Sankhla

23. Name the hypothesis that explains the spread of several species from North-east India along a once continuous central Indian mountain range into Western ghats, giving rise to several biological linkages between Western ghats and North East:
    (a) Hora hypothesis (b) Setna hypothesis (c) Raman hypothesis (d) None of the above

24. Identify this place where, due to proposed series of dams, the reed forests supplying the raw-material to over 300,000 basket and mat weavers is threatened to drown:
    (a) Bharatpur (b) Chilka (c) Poyamkooty (d) Jaisamand

25. Which of the following grass poses danger to wetlands due to restriction on grazing at Keoladeo Ghana National Park, Bharatpur?
    (a) *Paspalum distichum* (b) *Dicanthium annulatum*
    (c) *Heteropogon contortus* (d) None of the above

2

NATIONAL PARKS AND WILDLIFE SANCTUARIES

26. Name the sanctuary where one of the twelve holiest of holies (Jyotirlingam) temple is situated and sanctuary so named:
    (a) Bhimasankar (b) Pench (c) Kavera (d) Bori
27. Which sanctuary harbours a local endemic race of giant squirrel *Ratufa indica elphenstoni?*
    (a) Bhimasankar (b) Anamalai (c) Perambiculum
    (d) Kalakad
28. Name the biogeographic zone of India that sustains the largest number of endangered species of animals:
    (a) Deccan peninsula (b) Himalaya (c) Trans-Himalaya (d) North-East
29. "There are floating islands on lakes in Kashmir, Burma and North America that I have heard of, but I think that . . . this . . . is the only floating wildlife sanctuary in the world"—Thus wrote E.P. Gee in his book *The Wildlife of India.* Which National Park is he referring to?
    (a) Keibul Lamjao (b) Wular (c) Dachigam
    (d) Periyar

30. Name the species protected in the Keibul Lamjao National Park of Manipur:
(a) Thamin (*Cervus eldi*) (b) Hangul (*Cervus elaphus hanglu*) (c) Chital (*Axis axis*) (d) Musk Deer (*Moschus moschiferus*)

31. In which protected area has reintroduction of Grey Hornbills (*Tockus birostris*) and Black Bucks (*Antilope cervicapra*) been done simultaneously, for these species formerly occurred but have now disappeared from the area?
(a) Gir (b) Kanha (c) Sariska (d) Ranthambhore

32. Name the last refuge of the Asiatic Lion (*Panthera leo persica*) in the wild:
(a) Periyar National Park (b) Madhav National Park (c) Kaziranga National Park (d) Gir National Park

33. You have to name this National Park which originated as a game reserve and then further developed to preserve the watershed area for drinking water supply of Srinagar. It now covers an area of 141 sq. km and is famous as the last home of viable population of Hangul (*Cervus elaphus hanglu*):
(a) Dachigam National Park (b) Keibul Lamjao National Park (c) Salim Ali National Park (d) Indira Gandhi National Park

34. To which species of deer does Dachigam National Park serve as the last refuge?
(a) Hangul (*Cervus elaphus hanglu*) (b) Sambhar (*Cervus unicolor*) (c) Chital (*Axis axis*) (d) None of the above

35. A second attempt to reintroduce Asiatic Lion (*Panthera leo persica*) is being resorted to by

protecting and managing the potential area on the lines of the Gir National Park and it is proposed to introduce lions when habitat becomes suitable. This area has been notified as the wildlife sanctuary in the year 1979. Name this place:

(a) Chandraprabha Sanctuary (b) Barda Sanctuary (c) Madhav National Park (d) Ranthambhore National Park

36. Gene sanctuary is a protected area where plants of specific genetic materials and characteristics are found. Name one gene sanctuary created for an insectivorous plant:

(a) Nepenthes Sanctuary (Khasi hills) (b) Kanger Valley National Park, M.P. (c) Bori Sanctuary, M.P. (d) Sagarmatta National Park, Nepal

37. Name this proposed biosphere reserve where unique ecotone of teak (*Tectona grandis*) and Sal (*Shorea robusta*) forests exist and the famous Kotamsar caves (250 m long) with stalactites and stalagmites are found:

(a) Nokrek (b) Nilgiris (c) Kanger Valley (d) Bandhavgarh

38. Which Tiger Reserve forms a linking corridor for elephants (*Elephas maximus*) migrating between the forests of Bhutan and Manas Tiger Reserve in Assam?

(a) Kaziranga (b) Buxa (c) Namdapha (d) None of the above

39. Name a protected area created to protect primarily the remarkable flora of one part of India. Other animals found include Himalayan

Tahr (*Hemitragus jemlahicus*) and Musk Deer (*Moschus moschiferus*):
(a) Kalakad Sanctuary (b) Rajaji National Park (c) Valley of Flowers (d) Bandipur National Park

40. Which wetland in India has been created by a Maharaja as a shooting preserve for wildfowl. It now serves as the winter refuge for White Siberian Crane (*Grus leucogeranus*)?
(a) Keoladeo Ghana (b) Ranganthittu (c) Vedanthangal (d) Chilka

41. India's largest tiger reserve is approximately 3,500 sq. km. Name this Tiger Reserve:
(a) Periyar (b) Bandipur (c) Kanha (d) Nagarjunasagar

42. In the year 1979 an area in Nepal was declared a World Heritage Site and became eligible for funds from the UNESCO. It comprises Everest, Choster and Chooyu peaks of Nepal. Name this protected area:
(a) Royal Chitwan National Park (b) Khaptad National Park (c) Lake Rara National Park (d) Sagarmatta National Park

43. In South India a unique corridor of four protected areas is found. Three of these are Bandipur (Karnataka), Mudumalai Wildlife Sanctuary (Tamil Nadu), and Wynaad Wildlife Sanctuary of Kerala. Which is the fourth protected area?
(a) Anamalai (b) Kalakad (c) Nagarhole (d) Periyar

44. Name the protected area in India with the largest collection of Gharials (*Gavialis gangeticus*):

(a) Barren Island (b) Katarniaghat (c) Coringa (d) Narcondam Island

45. Identify this Indian bio-geographic z ne which covers barely 5% of India's area, but sustains 27% of all the species of higher plants recorded in India:

(a) Trans-Himalaya (b) Indian Desert (c) Western Ghats (d) Gangetic plains

46. Currently the largest continuum of wilderness exists in Karnataka, Kerala and Tamil Nadu. It forms a contiguous stretch of over 200 sq km Name the protected area forming this belt:

(a) Nagarhole–Bandipur–Mudumalai–Wynaad
(b) Bandipur–Mudumalai–Wynaad
(c) Nagarhole–Mudumalai–Periyar–Wynaad
(d) None of the above

47. Which Tiger Reserve forms the southernmost range of the Tiger (*Panthera tigris tigris*) in the Indian subcontinent?

(a) Bandipur (b) Kalakad–Mundanthurai (c) Periyar (d) Nagarjunasagar

48. Name the 17th Tiger Reserve of India to be created under the Project Tiger:

(a) Kalakad–Mundanthurai (b) Bandipur (c) Indravati (d) Nagarhole

49. In which state is the 18th Tiger Reserve of India located?

(a) M.P. (b) U.P. (c) Bihar (d) Assam

50. Identify the protected area in India which sometimes has been referred as the N'Gorongoro; this protected area also houses one of the two sub-species of Indian Barasingha:

(a) Indravati National Park (b) Kanha National Park (c) Bandhavgarh National Park (d) Panna National Park

51. Following the criteria laid down by UNESCO, the Indian National Man and Biosphere Committee identified some sites to be declared as Biosphere Reserves. Name the Biosphere Reserve area which falls under more than two states:

(a) Nilgiris (b) Nokrek (c) Desert (d) Kanha

52. In which lake excessive inflow of water decreased the salinity levels changing the growth of alga and food availability and once abundantly occurring crustacean *Artemia salina* has totally disappeared from the water body?

(a) Sambhar Lake (b) Jaisamand Lake (c) Ramgarh Lake (d) Sukhna Lake

53. You have to name this sanctuary which is one of three islands on the River Kaveri, 1.6 km from the historic city of Seringapatnam:

(a) Bharatpur, Keoladeo Ghana (b) Sultanpur Bird Sanctuary (c) Nelapattu, A.P. (d) Ranganthittu Bird Sanctuary

54. In which protected area in India you find the 10th century rock images of the various incarnations of Lord Vishnu?

(a) Kanha National Park (b) Bandhavgarh National Park, M.P. (c) Achanakmar Sanctuary, M.P. (d) Nagarhole National Park, Karnataka

55. Name the protected area supplying about 20% of Bombay city's drinking water:

(a) Borivli National Park (b) Kumbalgarh Sanctuary (c) Eravikulum National Park (d) Valmiki Tiger Reserve

56. Name a protected area that lies between the Erramalai and Nallamalai ranges of Eastern Ghat and enjoys two breeding seasons for Great Indian Bustard (*Choriotis nigriceps*):

    (a) Nelapattu (b) Rollapadu (c) Karera (d) None

57. Name a Tiger Reserve that holds as many as twenty species of fauna which are listed under Schedule I in the IUCN Red Data Book:

    (a) Kalakad-Mundanthurai, Tamil Nadu (b) Dudhwa, U.P. (c) Kanha, M.P. (d) Manas, Assam

58. Which sanctuary in Uttar Pradesh was identified as the alternative home for the Asiatic Lion (*Panthera leo persica*) and in 1957 an attempt was made to translocate a few lions but the operation was not a success?

    (a) Chilla (b) Rajaji (c) Motichur (d) Chandraprabha

59. In which National Park you find a unique eleven-metre long statue of a reclining Lord Vishnu called *Shesh Saiya*?

    (a) Bandhavgarh National Park (b) Fossil National Park, Sahpura, M.P. (c) Indravati National Park, M.P. (d) Borivli National Park, Bombay

60. Name the place where exists the largest nesting site of the Greater Flamingo (*Phoenicopterus roseus*) in Asia:

    (a) Little Runn of Kutch (b) Great Runn of Kutch (c) Chilka Lake (d) Vedanthangal

61. Name the largest protected area in India:

(a) Kaziranga, Assam (b) Namdapha Tiger Reserve, Arunachal Pradesh (c) Great Indian Bustard Sanctuary, Maharashtra (d) Periyar Tiger Reserve, Kerala

62. Name the only protected area which holds four major cats—the Tiger (*Panthera tigris*), the Leopard (*Panthera pardus*), the clouded Leopard (*Neofelis nebulosa*) and the snow Leopard (*Panthera uncia*):
(a) Namdapha National Park, Arunachal (b) Sagarmatta National Park, Nepal (c) Kaziranga National Park (d) Valley of Flowers National Park

63. Based on the study of which National Park, two books—*The Face of the Tiger* by C. McDougal and *The Heart of the Jungle* by K.K. Gurung—were published?
(a) Royal Chitwan, Nepal (b) Karnali Wildlife Reserve (c) Langtang National Park (d) Khaptad National Park

64. In which state is the Kumbalgarh Sanctuary—famous for the wolf breeding—situated?
(a) Tamil Nadu (b) M.P. (c) Rajasthan (d) Haryana

65. Name the protected area which was created in the year 1977 to protect Andaman Teal and Nicobar Pigeon:
(a) North Reef Island Sanctuary (b) Barren Island Sanctuary (c) Jarwa Tribal Reserve (d) None

66. Which National Park is the eastern limit of distribution of Chital (*Axis axis*) in India?

(a) Buxa, Bengal (b) Namdapha, Arunachal (c) Manas, Assam (d) Kaziranga, Assam

67. Which National Park in India has the largest population of swamp deer (*Cervus duvaceli*)?
(a) Kanha, M.P. (b) Rajaji, U.P. (c) Dudhwa, U.P. (d) Corbett, U.P.

68. Which National Park has the highest peak of South India—the Anaimudi 2695 m/8853 feet?
(a) Bandipur, Karnataka (b) Mudumalai, Tamil Nadu (c) Eraviculum, Kerala (d) Wynaad, Kerala

69. Which state was to establish India's first Marine National Park, Pirotan?
(a) Gujarat (b) Orissa (c) Tamil Nadu (d) Kerala

70. Name the biogeographical zone of India where the largest number of wild sheep and goats in the world are found:
(a) Trans-Himalaya (b) Gangetic Plain (c) Western Ghats (d) Islands

71. Name the biogeographic region having a network of wetlands, 20 species of turtle, two species of crocodile, Dolphin and Bengal Florican in good numbers:
(a) Trans-Himalaya (b) Western Ghats (c) Himalaya (d) Gangetic Plain

72. Which biogeographic zone in India has the highest percentage of protected area?
(a) Semi-arid (b) North-East India (c) Deccan Peninsula (d) Western Ghats

73. A state in India with 7300 sq. km area has only one National Park which occupies ten per cent of the land. This National Park protects many species of orchids and animals like tahr, musk

deer, serrow and snow leopard, etc. Which is this National Park?
(a) Kangchendzonga (b) Molem (c) Nauradehi (d) Dandeli

74. Name India's 18th Tiger Reserve which adjoins the Chitwan National Park in Nepal:
(a) Dudhwa (b) Corbett (c) Buxa (d) Valmiki

75. Name one protected area in India which has been created in the name of a primitive tribe to protect and safeguard the civilization and culture of these people:
(a) Jarwa Tribal Reserve (b) Kol Reserve (c) Naga Reserve (d) Onges Reserve

76. Name a protected area that holds the viable population of wild buffalo (*Bubalus bubalis*) in Central India and is a potential alternative home for the swamp deer (*Cervus duvaceli branderi*) of Kanha:
(a) Bandhavgarh National Park (b) Pench National Park (c) Indravati National Park (d) Tadoba National Park

77. Which protected area unit currently holds the largest protected population of Asian Elephant (*Elephas maximus*)?
(a) Dudhwa-Chitwan (b) Manas-Buxa (India) Manas (Bhutan) (c) Nagarhole-Bandipur-Mudumalai-Wynaad (d) Bandhavgarh

78. Which protected area in Indian subcontinent contains the largest concentration of Tigers?
(a) Kanha (b) Sundarbans (c) Kaziranga (d) Simlipal

79. In which protected area you still see the site of khedda method of elephant capture in Karnataka?
(a) Dandeli Sanctuary (b) Nagarhole/Bandipur National Park (c) Bannerghatta Sanctuary (d) Mookambika Sanctuary

80. Which is the largest zoological park in India?
(a) Arignar Anna Zoological Park (b) Alipore Zoological Garden (c) Trivandrum Zoological Garden (d) Allen Forest Zoo, Kanpur

81. Where is the oldest zoo in India situated?
(a) Allen Forest, Kanpur (b) Trivandrum Zoological Garden (c) National Zoological Park, Delhi (d) None of the above

82. Which protected area is a prime habitat for the Andaman Wild Pig (*Sus scrofa andamanensis*)?
(a) Middle Button Island National Park (b) Narcondam Island Sanctuary (c) Saddle Peak National Park (d) Mount Harriet National Park

83. Narcondam Island Sanctuary protects sole habitat of the Narcondam hornbill (*Rhytidoceros narcondami*). In which state is the sanctuary situated?
(a) Uttar Pradesh (b) Madhya Pradesh (c) Andaman and Nicobar Island (d) Andhra Pradesh

84. In the delta region of which river is the Coringa Sanctuary situated?
(a) Krishna (b) Kaveri (c) Godavari (d) Mahanadi

85. Name a protected area situated near the borders of Maharashtra, Madhya Pradesh and Andhra

Pradesh protecting the tiger, leopard, sloth bear, chinkara, mouse deer and leopard cat, etc.:
(a) Eturnagaram Sanctuary, Andhra Pradesh
(b) Pench National Park, Madhya Pradesh
(c) Nawegaon Sanctuary (d) None of the above

86. Which is the largest Tiger Reserve in India?
(a) Kanha (b) Dudhwa (c) Nagarjunasagar Srisailam (d) Indravati

87. Neelapattu Sanctuary in Andhra Pradesh is famous for which group of Fauna?
(a) Mammals (b) Ground birds (c) Water birds (d) Snakes

88. In which state is the Pakhal Sanctuary situated?
(a) Arunachal Pradesh (b) West Bengal (c) Andhra Pradesh (d) Assam

89. From which source does the Papikonda Sanctuary in Andhra Pradesh derive its name?
(a) Papikonda hill range (b) Papikonda lake (c) Papikonda river (d) Papikonda town

90. Which two states in India share the boundary of Pulicat Sanctuary for waterbirds?
(a) Andhra–Tamil Nadu (b) Andhra–Karnataka (c) Andhra–Kerala (d) Andhra–Maharashtra

91. Which tiger reserve forms the north-eastern limit of the Indian tigers' (*Panthera tigris tigris*) range?
(a) Kaziranga (b) Namdapha (c) Manas (d) Buxa

92. In which state is the Lali Sanctuary situated?
(a) Kerala (b) M.P. (c) Maharashtra (d) Arunachal Pradesh

93. In which state is the Pranhita Sanctuary situated?

(a) Bihar (b) Mizoram (c) Rajasthan (d) Andhra Pradesh

94. In which sanctuary you may see the hispid hare (*Caprolagus hispidus*)?
(a) Periyar National Park (b) Barnadi Wildlife Sanctuary (c) Bhimbandh Sanctuary (d) Bori Sanctuary

95. In which state is the Sonai Rupai Sanctuary situated?
(a) Assam (b) Meghalaya (c) Manipur (d) Tripura

96. Bhimbandh, Dalma and Gautam Buddha Sanctuaries are situated in which of the following states?
(a) Bihar (b) M.P. (c) U.P. (d) West Bengal

97. Which sanctuary is situated in the Uttar Pradesh and Bihar borders?
(a) Kaimur (b) Lawalong (c) Mahuadaur (d) Dalma

98. Udaipur Sanctuary is a six sq km wetland. In which state is it situated?
(a) Bihar (b) Rajasthan (c) Gujarat (d) Punjab

99. In which state are situated the Molem, Bondla and Coligao sanctuaries?
(a) Bihar (b) Assam (c) Maharashtra (d) Goa

100. In which state is the Bhagwan Mahavir National Park situated?
(a) Goa (b) Kerala (c) Manipur (d) Bihar

101. Name the state which is the last refuge of the Asiatic Lion (*Panthera leo persica*) and Indian Wild Ass (*Equus hemionus khur*):
(a) Gujarat (b) Rajasthan (c) Karnataka (d) Tamil Nadu

102. Which sanctuary was once occupied by Asiatic Lions but now lacks forest corridor to link it to Gir National Park?
(a) Dhrangadhra (b) Jessore (c) Barda (d) Nal Sarvovar

103. In which sanctuary you see the Indian Wild Ass?
(a) Dhrangadhra Sanctuary (b) Little Rann of Kutch (c) Both a & b (d) None of the above

104. In which state is Nal Sarovar Sanctuary situated?
(a) Rajasthan (b) Gujarat (c) Goa (d) Orissa

105. Velavadar National Park is famous for which animal?
(a) Black Buck (*Antilope cervicapra*)
(b) Asiatic Lion (*Panthera leo persica*)
(c) Indian Tiger (*Panthera tigris*)
(d) Goral (*Nemorhaedus goral*)

106. Dhumkhal Sanctuary of Gujarat is famous for which of the following animals?
(a) Sloth Bear (*Melursus ursinus*)
(b) Black Buck (*Antilope cervicapra*)
(c) Nilgai (*Bubalus bubalis*)

107. In which state is the Sultanpur Bird Sanctuary situated?
(a) Punjab (b) Gujarat (c) Uttar Pradesh (d) Haryana

108. If you visit the Chail Sanctuary what species of bird you are likely to see in big enclosure?
(a) Chir Pheasant (*Catreus wallichi*) (b) Blood Pheasant (*Ithaginis cruentus*) (c) Red Jungle Fowl (*Gallus gallus*) (d) Koklas Pheasant (*Pucrasia macrolopha*)

109. Where is the Great Himalayan National Park situated?
(a) Jammu & Kashmir (b) Himachal Pradesh
(c) Uttar Pradesh (d) North-Eastern states

110. Daran Ghati, Govind Sagar, Kalatop Khajjiar, Kanwar and Kugti Sanctuaries are situated in which part of India?
(a) Deccan peninsula (b) Himalayas (c) Thar Desert (d) Western Coast

111. Which of the following protected areas is the last refuge of Hangul (*Cervus elaphus hanglu*)?
(a) Dachigam National Park (b) Keibul Lamjao National Park (c) Hemis High Altitude National Park (d) Bandipur National Park

112. In which state is the Overa Sanctuary and proposed Overa-Aro Biosphere Reserve situated?
(a) Assam (b) Manipur (c) Tripura (d) Jammu & Kashmir

113. In which state is Biligiri Rangasamy Sanctuary situated?
(a) Karnataka (b) Kerala (c) Tamil Nadu (d) Andhra Pradesh

114. In which state are the Mookambika, Dandeli, Brahmagiri and Ghataprabha sanctuaries situated?
(a) Karnataka (b) Kerala (c) Tamil Nadu (d) Goa

115. Ranibennur Sanctuary is famous for which of the following animals?
(a) Black Buck (*Antilope cervicapra*)
(b) Wolf (*Canis lupus*)
(c) Great Indian Bustard (*Choriotis nigriceps*)
(d) All the above

116. Name the sanctuary that stretches around the Parambiculum, Thunacadavu and Peruvaripallan dams:
(a) Eraviculum (b) Parambiculum (c) Neyyar (d) Peppara

117. Which sanctuary holds the rare bird species such as Ceylon Frogmouth (*Batrachostomus moniliger*) and it is also the first bird sanctuary of Kerala?
(a) Thattekkad (b) Peechi Vazhani (c) Wynaad (d) Parambiculum

118. Which sanctuary in Kerala shares common borders with Nagarhole and Bandipur National Parks in Karnataka and Mudumalai Sanctuary in Tamil Nadu?
(a) Barnawapara (b) Wynaad (c) Peppara (d) Thattekkad

119. Karera Sanctuary in Madhya Pradesh is famous for which animal?
(a) Great Indian Bustard (*Choriotis nigriceps*)
(b) Leopard (*Panthera pardus*) (c) Sambhar (*Cervus unicolor*) (d) Wild Buffalo (*Bubalus bubalis*)

120. Which sanctuary was formed to protect the Gharial (*Gavialis gangeticus*) and streches across three states—Madhya Pradesh, Uttar Pradesh and Rajasthan?
(a) National Chambal Sanctuary
(b) Bhairamgarh (c) Bori Sanctuary
(d) Pachmarhi Sanctuary.

121. Name the National Park which was created in the year 1936 as India's first National Park:
(a) Corbett (b) Silent Valley (c) Bandipur (d) Pirotan

122. Corbett National Park of today was created in the year 1936 and the name given then was Haily National Park. In the year 1952 it was again renamed. In the year 1957 it was renamed as Corbett National Park. Give the name adopted during 1952 to 1957:
    (a) Kanha National Park (b) Ramganga National Park (c) Pirotan National Park (d) None of the above

123. Name the National Park in Maharashtra that shares the boundary with a National Park of same name in Madhya Pradesh:
    (a) Sanjay Gandhi National Park (b) Pench National Park (c) Melghat Tiger Reserve (d) Tadoba National Park

124. In which state are the Siju and Nongkhyllem Sanctuaries situated?
    (a) Assam (b) Meghalaya (c) Nagaland (d) Tripura

125. In which state are the Fakim and Itanki Sanctuaries situated?
    (a) Orissa (b) Nagaland (c) Rajasthan (d) West Bengal

126. Bhitarkanika Sanctuary in Orissa is famous for an animal, namely:
    (a) Estuarine Crocodile (*Crocodilus porosus)*
    (b) Gharial (*Gavialis gangeticus*) (c) Black Buck (*Antilope cervicapra*) (d) None of the above

127. Name a Sancutary in Orissa having a waterspread of 900 sq km famous for many species of migratory birds:
    (a) Ghana (b) Chilka (c) Balukhand (d) Baisipalli

128. In which state is the Satkosia Gorge Sanctuary situated?
(a) Tamil Nadu (b) Kerala (c) Karnataka (d) Orissa

129. In which state is the Similipal Tiger Reserve situated?
(a) Orissa (b) Maharashtra (c) Andhra Pradesh (d) Madhya Pradesh

130. Satkosia Gorge, now a Sanctuary, is formed due to action of which river?
(a) Kaveri (b) Krishna (c) Godavari (d) Mahanadi

131. Which Sanctuary from the following is *not* in Rajasthan?
(a) Bhensrodgarh (b) Darrah (c) Jaisamand (d) Achanakmar

132. Which Sanctuary includes the highest point of elevation in the Aravalli Hills?
(a) Ranthambhore (b) Mount Abu (c) Tal Chapper (d) Ramgarh

133. Which protected area is included in the 17th Tiger Reserve along with the Kalakad Sanctuary?
(a) Mudumali Sanctuary (b) Annamalai Sanctuary (c) Mundanthurai Sanctuary (d) Pulicat Sanctuary

134. In which state is the Point Calimere Sanctuary situated?
(a) Kerala (b) Karnataka (c) Tamil Nadu (d) Goa

135. In which state is the Katerniaghat Sanctuary situated?
(a) M.P. (b) Orissa (c) U.P. (d) Himachal Pradesh

136. Name the Sanctuary in West Bengal near Santiniketan of Rabindranath Tagore:
(a) Ballarpur (b) Mahananda (c) Sajnakhali (d) Gorumara
137. Which Sanctuary acts as a buffer zone to the Indravati National Park of M.P.?
(a) Achanakmar (b) Badaikhol (c) Pamed (d) Bhairamgarh
138. In which state is the Kanger Ghati National Park situated?
(a) M.P. (b) U.P. (c) Kerala (d) Bihar
139. In which state is the Melghat Tiger Reserve situated?
(a) Maharashtra (b) Madhya Pradesh (c) Bihar (d) Goa
140. Name a National Park in U.P. on which W. Smyth published a book way back in 1938:
(a) Nandadevi (b) Kedarnath (c) Valley of Flowers (d) Corbett

3

BOOKS AND AUTHORS

141. Billy Arjan Singh wrote four books as a result of study in the forests of Uttar Pradesh and Dudhwa National Park. These books are *Tiger Haven; Tara, A Tigress; Tiger Tiger.* Name the fourth book:
(a) *Fall of a Sparrow* (b) *The Snakeman* (c) *Tree Tops* (d) *The Prince of Cats*
142. Which book of Salim Ali is co-authored by S. Dillon Ripley?

(a) *The Birds of Kutch* (b) *Birds of Kerala* (c) *The Birds of Sikkim* (d) *The Handbook of the Birds of India and Pakistan*

143. Which book is *not* written by Dr Salim Ali?
   (a) *Birds of Kerala* (b) *The Birds of Sikkim* (c) *The Birds of Kutch* (d) *Tree Tops*

144. Which is the last book written by Jim Corbett?
   (a) *Tree Tops* (b) *Tiger Lady* (c) *Jungle and Backyard* (d) *The Tigers of Rajasthan*

145. Which book is *not* written by Jim Corbett?
   (a) *Man Eating Leopard of Rudraprayag* (b) *Jungle Lore* (c) *My India* (d) *Tiger*

146. Who wrote the books *Man-Eaters of Kumaon* and *The Temple Tiger*?
   (a) Corbett (b) Romulus Whitaker (c) Salim Ali (d) None of the above

147. Who is the author of the book *Field Guide to the Birds of Eastern Himalaya*?
   (a) Zai Whitaker (b) Romulus Whitaker (c) Salim Ali (d) S. Dillon Ripley

148. Who wrote the book *Birds of Andaman & Nicobar Islands*?
   (a) Salim Ali (b) Dr Tikader (c) S. Dillon Ripley (d) J.H. Dick

149. Who is the author of *The Twilight of India's Wildlife*?
   (a) Olive Smythies (b) B. Seshadri (c) M. Krishnan (d) Forsyth

150. Jim Corbett wrote, 'It is of these people, who are admittedly poor . . . among whom I have lived and whom I love, that I . . . tell in the pages of this book.' Which book is he referring to?

(a) *Tree Tops* (b) *Jungle Lore* (c) *My India* (d) *Born Free*

151. Currently who is the publisher for the books of Jim Corbett?
(a) Collins (b) Penguin India (c) Oxford University Press (d) Indian Wildlife Institute

152. *The Snake Man* is a biography of:
(a) Arjan Singh (b) Zai Whitaker (c) Romulus Whitaker (d) Jim Corbett

153. Who wrote the biographical work *The Snake Man?*
(a) Zai Whitaker (b) Romulus Whitaker (c) Joy Adamson (d) George Adamson

154. Whose autobiography is the *Fall of a Sparrow?*
(a) Salim Ali (b) A. A. Danber Brander (c) S. Dillon Ripley (d) Bernhard Grizemek

155. Who wrote the profusely illustrated book *Indian Wildlife* in the year 1984?
(a) Rajesh and Ramesh Bedi (b) Ramesh and Naresh Bedi (c) Rajesh and Naresh Bedi (d) None of them

156. Which book written by Guy Mountfort gives a survey of the Project Tiger in India?
(a) *Tigers* (b) *The Call of the Tiger* (c) *Tigerland* (d) *Tiger! The Story of the Indian Tiger.*

157. Who wrote the book *Tiger–Portrait of A Predator* published by Collins in 1986?
(a) S.P. Sahai (b) B. Seshadri (c) Samar Singh (d) Valmik Thapar & Fateh Singh Rathore

158. Who wrote the book *The Book of Indian Animals* which is an important reference book on the mammals of the Indian subcontinent?

(a) M.L. Roonwal (b) G.B. Schaller (c) S. Prater (d) Kailash Sankhala

159. Ajit Mukherjee wrote a book about endangered animals of India. What is the title of this book?
(a) *Extinct and Vanishing Birds and Mammals of India* (b) *Threatened Animals of India* (c) *Red Data Book* (d) *Greenfile*

160. Who wrote the book *Birds in India* in the year 1931?
(a) Salim Ali (b) A.O. Hume (c) R.S.P. Bates (d) S. Dillon Ripely

161. Who is the author of the book *A Guide to the Birds of the Delhi Area*?
(a) Usha Ganguli (b) Salim Ali (c) H.P.W. Hutson (d) Khuswant Singh

162. Who is the author of the book *The Birds about Delhi*?
(a) Usha Ganguli (b) S. Dillon Ripley (c) H.P.W. Hutson (d) Salim Ali

163. Who illustrated the book *A Pictorial Guide to the Birds of the Indian Subcontinent*?
(a) John Henry Dick (b) J. P. Irani (c) Wan Tho Loke (d) Martin Woodcock

164. Which book forms the basis for *The Handbook of the Birds of India and Pakistan* by Salim Ali and S. D. Ripley?
(a) *The Book of Indian Birds* (b) *A Synopsis of the Birds of India and Nepal* (c) *A Bundle of Feathers* (d) *The Birds of India*

165. Who is the author of the book *Search for the Spiny Babbler*—a book about the only endemic bird of Nepal?

(a) Salim Ali (b) S. Dillon Ripley (c) J. S. Serrao
(d) Zafer Futehally

166. Who wrote the book *With Tigers in the Wild?*
(a) W. Rice (b) T. C. Jerdon (c) Billy Arjan Singh
(d) Fateh Singh Rathore, Valmik Thapar & Tejbir Singh

167. Who wrote the book *Tiger* published by Collins in 1978?
(a) Kailash Sankhala (b) S. P. Shahi (c) V. B. Saharia (d) Jim Corbett

168. Who wrote the book *The Deer and the Tiger*—a study of Kanha National Park?
(a) Arjan Singh (b) A. M. Smith (c) G. B. Schaller (d) R. L. Sutton

169. Allen Huge wrote an account of central Madhya Pradesh in which of the following books?
(a) *The Lonely Tiger* (b) *My India* (c) *Tree Tops* (d) *Jungle Lore*

170. Who wrote the biography of the Jim Corbett titled *Carpet Sahib—A Life of Jim Corbett?*
(a) Jim Corbett (b) Martin Booth (c) R. G. Burton (d) J. Forsyth

171. Which organization publishes *The State of India's Environment?*
(a) B.N.H.S. (b) WWF–India (c) I.U.C.N.
(d) Centre for Science and Environment

172. Who wrote the book *The Sportsman's Book for India?*
(a) F.G.A. Aflalo (b) H. Allen (c) N. A. Baikov (d) E. B. Baker

173. Who wrote the book *India and Tiger Hunting?*
(a) J. Barras (b) E. H. Baxter (c) W. Baze (d) J. W. Best

174. Who is the author of the book *Wild Animals in Central India?*
(a) V. Brook (b) A. A. Danbar Brander (c) J. M. Brown (d) W. S. Burke

175. Who wrote the book *Blue Tiger?*
(a) T. Campbell (b) N. Carr (c) H. R. Caldwell (d) Corbett

176. Who wrote the book *The Highlands of Central India?*
(a) E.P. Gee (b) J. Forsyth (c) M. Y. Ghorpade (d) P. Hanley

177. Who wrote the book *The Wildlife of India?*
(a) E.P. Gee (b) Salim Ali (c) J.M. Brown (d) J. Corbett

178. Who is the author of *The Mammals of India?*
(a) T. C. Jerdon (b) D. Johnson (c) I. Khan (d) Joy Adamson

179. Who is the author of the book *Wild Animals of Indian Empire?*
(a) S. H. Prater (b) J. C. Daniel (c) Billy Arjan Singh (d) H. S. Panwar

180. P. J. Deoras and K. G. Ghorpurey wrote separately two books which bear the same title. What is the title of the book?
(a) *Snakes of India* (b) *Indian Snakes* (c) *Common Indian Snakes* (d) *The Book of Indian Reptiles*

181. Who is the author of *The Book of Indian Reptiles?*
(a) P. J. Deoras (b) E. Nicholson (c) Romulus Whitaker (d) J. C. Daniel

182. Who is the author of *Butterflies of India?*
(a) M. A. Wynter Blyth (b) M. S. Mani (c) C. Smith (d) C. B. Antram

183. Who wrote the book *Butterflies of the Indian Region?*
    (a) M. A. Wynter-Blyth (b) C. Smith (c) M. S. Mani (d) T. C. Jerdon

184. Who is the publisher of the famous insight guide *Indian Wildlife?*
    (a) B.N.H.S. (b) Oxford (c) Collins (d) APA Publications

185. Who is the author of the book *My Pride and Joy?*
    (a) George Adamson (b) Joy Adamson (c) Martin Booth (d) James Hancock

186. Who wrote the book *Common Birds* for National Book Trust of India?
    (a) Zafer Futehally (b) Laeeq Futehally (c) Tehmina Salim Ali (d) Salim Ali

187. What is the title of the nature magazine for children being published by the publishers of the *Sanctuary Asia* magazine?
    (a) *Cub* (b) *Pup* (c) *Nature* (d) *Wildlife*

188. From which city *Sanctuary Asia* is published?
    (a) Bombay (b) Delhi (c) Madras (d) Calcutta

189. Who is the author of *A Study of the Flora and Fauna of Bharatpur Bird Sanctuary?*
    (a) V. S. Saxena (b) V. B. Saharia (c) Rajpal Singh (d) James Hancock

190. Who wrote *Popular Handbook of Indian Birds?*
    (a) Salim Ali (b) Martin Woodcock (c) Hugh Whisler (d) Usha Ganguli

4

PERSONALITIES

191. Name the person who made the thrilling re-discovery of Jerdons' Double Banded Courser (*Cursorius bitorquatus*):
(a) Salim Ali (b) Tehmina Salim Ali (c) Bharat Bhusan (d) Bittu Sahgal

192. Salim Ali has been honoured with an award for which he is the only Indian recipient. Which is the award?
(a) Nobel Prize (b) Paul Getty Award for Conservation (c) Borlaug Award (d) Briksha Mitra Award

193. Name the person who gave the first news of existence of the Golden Langur (*Presbytis geei*) though he did not produce any evidence in his favour:
(a) E. P. Gee (b) E. O. Shebbeare (c) Jim Corbett (d) David Attenborough

194. Who wrote, 'The book of nature has no beginning as it has no end'?
(a) Jim Corbett (b) Mahatma Gandhi (c) Anil Aggarwal (d) Madhav Gadgil

195. Which emperor of India formulated laws for wildlife preservation?
(a) Ashoka (b) Akbar (c) Babur (d) None of the above

196. Who is responsible for getting the Dudhwa National Park established? To recognise his efforts he was honoured with World Wide Fund

for Nature International Gold Medal in the year 1976?
(a) Ram Lakhan Singh (b) H.S. Panwar (c) Kailash Sankhala (d) Arjan Singh

197. Who is the first Director of Wildlife Institute of India, Dehra Dun?
(a) R.V. Singh (b) J. B. Lal (c) H. S. Panwar (d) Samar Singh

198. Who rediscovered the Golden Gecko (*Calodactylodes aureus*)? It was last seen about 115 years ago.
(a) J. C. Daniel (b) S. A. Hussain (c) A. R. Rahmani (d) M. Krishnan

199. Where was the Golden Gecko (*Calodactylodes aureus*) re-discovered?
(a) Satpura Hills (b) Vindhya Hills (c) Tirupati Hills (d) Palni Hills

200. Name a tiger specialist who was a forester by profession and was instrumental in the preparation of management plan for Desert Biosphere Reserve:
(a) Kailash Sankhala (b) H. S. Panwar (c) Fateh Singh Rathore (d) Ram Lakhan Singh

201. What was the full name of the noted ornithologist Salim Ali?
(a) Abdul Moizuddin Salim Ali (b) Moizuddin Abdul Salim Ali (c) Salim Ali (d) Abdul Salim Ali

202. Who wrote this letter to Salim Ali: *It was an honor for me to be able to nominate you for the second J. Paul Getty Wildlife Conservation Prize. I want to thank you for winning and thereby causing my*

judgement to be confirmed by the distinguished International Jury.— Congratulations! ?

(a) Ronald Reagan (b) George Bush (c) Rockefeller (d) Charles McMathias

203. Who is the founder of the Madras Snake Park?
(a) Romulus Whitaker (b) J. C. Daniel (c) Tamil Nadu Government (d) None of the above

204. Romulus Whitaker is an authority in the field of:
(a) Snakes (b) Birds (c) Mammals (d) Frogs

5

WILDLIFE CONSERVATION IN INDIA

205. National Wildlife Action Plan of India derives inspiration from three main sources—first, the World Conservation Strategy 1980, second, Bali Action Plan 1982. Name the third one:
(a) World Charter for Nature (b) Corbett Action Plan (c) Ramsar Convention (d) World Heritage Convention

206. In which year was the World Charter for Nature adopted by the U.N. General Assembly?
(a) 29 October, 1981 (b) 29 October, 1982 (c) 29 October, 1983 (d) 29 October, 1984.

207. In the year 1985 between 3 and 8 February, representatives of 12 Asian countries got together in India and formulated an Action Plan for the Protected Areas of Indo-Malayan Realm. What is the popular name of this Action Plan?

(a) Bali Action Plan (b) Corbett Action Plan (c) National Wildlife Action Plan (d) None of the above

208. The Corbett Action Plan 1985 refers to the protection of which Realm?
(a) Indo-Malayan (d) Indo-Chinese (c) Indo-Sri Lankan (d) Indo-Siamese

209. Indo-Malayan Realm is subdivided into 4 sub-regions. These are Indian, Indo-Chinese, Wallacean and:
(a) Chinese sub-region (b) Sri Lankan sub-region (c) Sundaic sub-region (d) Baltic sub-region

210. Name the country which was the venue for the launch of the World Conservation Strategy:
(a) Pakistan (b) Switzerland (c) Brazil (d) India

211. When was the World Conservation Strategy launched?
(a) 6 March, 1980 (b) 6 March, 1984 (c) 6 March, 1982 (d) 6 March, 1990

212. The task force on 'eliciting public support for wildlife conservation' was set up in pursuance of the recommendations of the Indian Board for Wildlife and its standing committee at their meeting held on 9 February, 1981, and 1 July, 1982, gave a term SAED. What does it mean?
(a) Special Areas for Eco-Development (b) Strategy Against Eco-Destruction (c) Specific Action for Economic Development (d) Special Areas for Economic Development

213. Which convention was the first to aim at a worldwide participation and to concern itself exclusively with habitat?

(a) Bonn Convention (b) Ramsar Convention (c) Whaling Convention (d) World Heritage Convention

214. The Convention on Wetlands of International Importance especially as Waterfowl Habitat was signed on 2 February, 1971, in an Iranian town and came into force on 21 December, 1985. Give the name by which the convention is commonly known:

(a) Ramsar Convention (b) Wetland Convention (c) Iranian Convention (d) Waterfowl Convention

215. Is India a party to the Ramsar Convention?

(a) Yes (b) No

216. The Convention on the Conservation of Migratory Species of Wild Animals was signed on 23 June, 1979, and came into force on 1 November, 1983. What is the popular name given to this Convention?

(a) Bonn Convention (b) Ramsar Convention (c) Bird Convention (d) No popular name

217. Is India a party to the Bonn Convention?

(a) Yes (b) No

218. Is India a party to the Convention concerning the protection of the World Cultural and Natural Heritage?

(a) Yes (b) No

219. The Convention concerning the protection of the World Cultural and Natural Heritage was adopted at the General Conference of the UNESCO on 16 November, 1972. When did it come into force?

(a) 17 December, 1972 (b) 17 December, 1975
(c) 16 December, 1973 (d) 16 December, 1974

220. What is the popular name given to the Convention concerning the protection of the World Cultural and Natural Heritage?
(a) Cultural Convention (b) Natural Convention (c) World Heritage Convention (d) No popular name

221. India, besides being a party to big four Wildlife Conventions, has also signed a bilateral migratory bird treaty with one country:
(a) Pakistan (b) Afghanistan (c) USSR (d) USA

222. CCAMLR was signed in Canberra in May 1980 and came into force on 7 April, 1982. For which area is this convention meant?
(a) Antarctica (b) Asia (c) Amazonia (d) Arctic

223. Red Data Book is the term applied to the book dealing with which data?
(a) Threatened and rare species of plants
(b) Threatened and rare species of animals
(c) (a) and (b) both (d) Species of animals out of danger

224. What is the name given to the book which contains the names of the rare plants growing in botanical gardens and protected areas?
(a) Red Data Book (b) Green Book (c) Yellow Data Book (d) Green File

225. Which is the fourth convention in the family of 'big four' Conventions besides Ramsar Convention, World Heritage Convention and Bonn Convention?
(a) Convention on International Trade of Endangered Species of Fauna and Flora

(b) Whaling Convention (c) Bird Convention (d) None of the above

226. What kind of habitats are listed in Ramsar List?
(a) Boreal Forests (b) Wetlands (c) Deserts (d) Coniferous Forests

227. What is the name given to a wetland included under the Convention on Wetlands of International Importance especially as Waterfowl Habitats?
(a) Ramsar Site (b) Waterfowl Site (c) Ramsar Wetland (d) Wetland

228. The earliest effort in listing the rare and endangered plant Taxa of India was made in 1970 and about one hundred species were listed. Besides the Botanical Survey of India, which institution was involved in this task?
(a) Forest Research Institute, Dehra Dun (b) Institute of Deciduous Forests, Jabalpur (c) Institute of Rain and Moist Deciduous Forest Research, Jorhat (d) Institute of Forest Genetics and Tree Breeding, Coimbatore

229. When was the Wildlife (Protection) Act passed in India?
(a) 1972 (b) 1974 (c) 1976 (d) 1982

230. In which year was the Elephant Preservation Act passed by the British Government in India?
(a) 1879 (b) 1876 (c) 1857 (d) 1927

231. In which year the Bengal Rhinoceros Act was passed?
(a) 1931 (b) 1932 (c) 1941 (d) 1972

232. In which year was the Wild Birds and Wild Animals (Protection) Act passed in India?
(a) 1912 (b) 1810 (c) 1910 (d) 1919

233. In India perhaps the first Act exclusively for the habitat protection was the Hailey National Park Act of Uttar Pradesh, under which the Hailey National Park (now Corbett National Park) was set up. In which year this Act was passed?
(a) 1936 (b) 1946 (c) 1956 (d) 1966

234. In which year was the Project Tiger launched to save the Indian Tiger (*Panthera tigris*) from extinction?
(a) 1972 (b) 1973 (c) 1974 (d) 1982

235. In India, in the year 1970 which major conservation project was launched?
(a)) Project Hangul (b) Crocodile Breeding Project (c) Project Tiger (d) Project Elephant

236. In the year 1975 which conservation project was launched as joint effort of the Government of India, FAO and UNDP?
(a) Project Hangul (b) Crocodile Breeding and Management Project (c) Gir Lion Sanctuary Project (d) None of the above

237. Where is the Central Crocodile Breeding and Management Institute situated?
(a) Hyderabad (b) Madras (c) Calcutta (d) Satna

238. At the IUCN meetings in the year 1969 and 1972 critical status of a species of big cat was recognised and the Gujarat government started a protection project. Name this project:
(a) Gir Lion Sanctuary Project (b) Black Buck Project (c) Cat Project (d) Project Tiger

239. In which state(s) is the Himalayan Musk Deer Ecology and Conservation Project operating?
(a) Himachal Pradesh, J & K and U.P. (b) Jammu & Kashmir (c) Uttar Pradesh (d) U.P. and J & K

240. Besides Project Hangul and Himalayan Musk Deer Ecology and Conservation Project which is the other project to protect a species of deer in India?
(a) Manipur Brow-Antlered Deer Conservation Project (b) Project Sambhar (c) Project Cheetal (d) Project Goral

241. Where is the Institute of Forest Genetics and Tree Breeding located?
(a) Bangalore (b) Madras (c) Coimbatore (d) Jabalpur

242. Where is the Institute of Wood Science and Technology located?
(a) Bangalore (b) Jabalpur (c) Bhopal (d) Satna

243. Where is the Institute of Deciduous Forests located?
(a) Jabalpur (b) Jorhat (c) Calcutta (d) Pune

244. Where is the Institute of Arid Zone Forestry Research located?
(a) Jodhpur (b) Udaipur (c) Jaipur (d) Bikaner

245. Where is the Institute of Rain and Moist Deciduous Forest Research located?
(a) Jammu (b) Jorhat (c) Trivandrum (d) Port Blair

246. Where is the Forest Research Institute located?
(a) Dehra Dun (b) Bhopal (c) Bombay (d) Mussoorie

247. Where is the Indian Institute of Forest Management located?
(a) Bombay (b) Bhopal (c) Jabalpur (d) Peechi

248. Where is the Wildlife Institute of India located?
(a) Jorhat (b) Mussoorie (c) Coimbatore (d) Dehra Dun

249. Where are the headquarters of the Forest Survey of India located?
(a) Shimla (b) Dehra Dun (c) Mysore (d) Ahmedabad

250. Where is the Centre for Science and Environment located?
(a) New Delhi (b) Jaipur (c) Udaipur (d) Cochin

251. Where is the Central Soil and Water Conservation Research Centre located?
(a) Dehra Dun (b) Bhopal (c) Pune (d) Lucknow

252. Where is the Central Arid Zone Research Institute located?
(a) Jaipur (b) Jodhpur (c) Udaipur (d) Bharatpur

253. Where is the Indian Grassland and Fodder Research Institute located?
(a) Ooty (b) Bombay (c) Jhansi (d) Pune

254. Where are the headquarters of the National Bureau of Plant Genetic Resources located?
(a) New Delhi (b) Bhopal (c) Mysore (d) Raipur

255. Where is the National Environmental Engineering Research Institute located?
(a) Kolhapur (b) Bombay (c) Nagpur (d) Pune

256. Where are the headquarters of B.N.H.S. located?
(a) Bombay (b) Nagpur (c) Hyderabad (d) Satna

257. Where are the headquarters of the World Wide Fund for Nature—India located?
(a) Bombay (b) Nagpur (c) Madras (d) Calcutta

258. Where is the Indira Gandhi National Forest Academy—a training institution for officers of the Indian Forest Service—located?
(a) Mussoorie (b) Dehra Dun (c) Coimbatore (d) Burnihat

259. Where are the headquarters of the Data Centre for Natural Resources located?
(a) Delhi (b) Bhopal (c) Bangalore (d) Madras

6

THE MAMMALS

260. Name a cream-coloured Langur named after tea-planter naturalist E.P. Gee who provided in 1953 the evidence of existence of this animal.
(a) Hollock Gibbon (*Hylobates hoolock)*
(b) Bonnet Macaque (*Macaca radiata)*
(c) Rhesus Macaque (*Macaca mulatta*)
(d) Golden Langur (*Presbytes geei*)

261. Name the Macaque having a bonnet of long hairs radiating in all directions from a whorl on the crown of the head:
(a) Bonnet Macaque (*Macaca radiata*)
(b) Nilgiri Langur (*Presbytis Johni*)
(c) Assamese Macaque (*Macaca assamensis*)
(d) None of the above

262. Which is the only ape in India?
(a) Hollock or Whitebrowed Gibbon (*Hylobates hoolock*) (b) Liontailed Macaque (*Macaca silenus*) (c) Common Langur (*Presbytes entellus*) (d) None

263. Which monkey has the crown of erect and coarse hairs directed backwards from the forehead?

(a) Capped Langur (*Presbytes pileatus*)
(b) Golden Langur (*Presbytes geei*) (c) Nilgiri
Langur (*Presbytes Johni*) (d) None

264. Capped Langur (*Presbytes pileatus*) is also known as:
(a) Leaf Monkey (b) Hanuman Monkey
(c) Stumptailed Macaque (d) No alternative name

265. Name a black-coloured Langur found in the Western Ghats and hill ranges of Nilgiris, Annamalai, Brahmagiri, and Palani:
(a) Nilgiri Langur (*Presbytes Johni*)
(b) Liontailed Macaque (*Macaca silenus*)
(c) Common Langur (*Presbytes entellus*) (d) No Langur found in south India

266. Name a black or brownish black coloured Macaque found in the Western Ghats:
(a) Nilgiri Langur (*Presbytes Johni*)
(b) Liontailed Macaque (*Macaca silenus*)
(c) Slow Loris (*Nycticebus coucang*) (d) None

267. Which is the only tailless primate other than the Hollock Gibboon (*Hylobates hoolock*) in India?
(a) Bonnet Macaque (*Macaca radiata*)
(b) Slender Loris (*Loris tardigradus*) (c) Nilgiri Langur (*Presbytes Johni*) (d) None

268. Which is an endemic Langur of the Manas Tiger Reserve?
(a) Golden Langur (*Presbytes geei*) (b) Nilgiri Langur (*Presbytes Johni*) (c) Capped Langur (*Presbytes pileatus*) (d) No endemic Langur in Manas

269. Which animal in India is called the Hanuman Langur?
   (a) Leaf Monkey (*Presbytes pileatus*)
   (b) Common Langur (*Presbytes entellus*)
   (c) Rhesus Macaque (*Macaca mulatta*)
   (d) Assamese Macaque (*Macaca assamensis*)

270. In which biogeographic zone you find the Stumptailed Macaque (*Macaca arctoides*) and Pigtailed Macaque (*M. nemestrina*)?
   (a) North-east (b) Deccan Peninsula
   (c) Islands (d) Coasts

271. How many species of primates are found in the Indian subcontinent?
   (a) 10 (b) 21 (c) 40 (d) 35

272. Of the three groups of monkey found in the Indian subcontinent Macaques are represented by maximum number of species. How many species of Macaques are found in our region?
   (a) 8   (b) 12   (c) 6   (d) 9

273. What is the group of a monkey called?
   (a) Troop   (b) Herd (c) School   (d) Flock

274. Which Macaque in India has the mane of long dark grey hairs?
   (a) Liontailed Macaque (*Macaca silenus*)
   (b) Stumptailed Macaque (*M. arctoides*)
   (c) Pigtailed Macaque (*M. nemestrina*)
   (d) Longtailed Macaque (*M. fasciacularis*)

275. How many Genera of Loris are found in India?
   (a) 2   (b) 4   (c) 5   (d) 9

276. How many races of Tiger (*Panthera tigris*) are recognized in the world?

(a) 8   (b) 7   (c) 16   (d) 2

277. Of the eight races of Tiger in the world how many are extinct?
(a) 2   (b) 4   (c) 1   (d) None

278. What is the place of origin of the Tiger?
(a) Sumatra (b) Java   (c) Siberia   (d) India

279. Which of the following races of the Tiger (*Panthera tigris*) are extinct?
(a) Caspian Tiger (*P.t. virgata*) (b) Bali Tiger (*P.t. baltica*) (c) Javan Tiger (*P.t. sondaica*) (d) Only (a) and (b) are extinct

280. What was the name given to White Tiger trapped in the forests of Rewa, Madhya Pradesh?
(a) Mohan (b) Sohan (c) Johan (d) Champa

281. Of the 8 races of the Tiger (*Panthera tigris*) which one is the typical tiger (*P.t. tigris*)?
(a) Indian (b) Chinese (c) Sumatran (d) Bali

282. The first organised census of the Asiatic Lion (*Panthera leo persica*) was held in Gir Forests in 1936 and a total number concluded was 287. What was the census method followed?
(a) Pugmark census   (b) Capture and release method (c) Transect sampling   (d) None of the above.

283. For lions in India after carrying out the pugmark census in 1936, 1950 and 1963, M. K. Dalvi, IFS, then Conservator of Forests, decided to change the census method. What method he applied for the census?
(a) Waterhole census (b) Direct visual count
(c) Capture and release   (d) None

284. What is the social group of the lions called?

(a) Herd (b) Troop (c) Sounders (d) Pride

285. Currently how many races (sub-species) of Lion are living?
(a) 2   (b) 3   (c) 1   (d) 5

286. Which one of the following animals is extinct?
(a) Asiatic Lion   (b) African Lion
(c) Barbary Lion (d) None of the above

287. What is the gestation period of Asiatic Lion (*Panthera leo persica*)?
(a) 116 days (b) 130 days
(c) 40 days   (d) 200 days

288. Which species of cat in India has non-retractile claws?
(a) Asiatic Lion (*Panthera leo persica*) (b) Indian Tiger (*Panthera tigris tigris*) (c) Indian Cheetah (*Acinonyx jubatus venaticus*) (d) Pallas's Cat (*Felis manul*)

289. Is it true that cubs of the Lion (*Panthera leo*) are spotted when young?
(a) Yes (b) No

290. In his autobiography Salim Ali writes, 'A brother of Maharaja Surguja has earned unenviable immortality by sportingly gunning down all of the three last remaining . . . wild individuals of this species in a single night and thus successfully wiping out the species for all time from India.' To which species is Salim Ali referring?
(a) Pallas's Cat (*Felis manul*) (b) Lynx (*Felis lynx*) (c) Indian Cheetah (*Acinonyx jubatus*) (d) Asiatic Lion (*Panthera leo*)

291. During the prehistoric times from which route the Cheetah migrated into India?
(a) South-east pass   (b) North-west pass
(c) Northern pass   (d) None of the above

292. What is a Hunting Leopard?
(a) Cheetah (*Acinonyx jubatus*) (b) Snow Leopard (*Panthera uncia*) (c) Panther (*Panthera pardus*) (d) None of the above

293. Which animal known for its playfulness was used by Indian princes for hunting till as late as the middle of this century when it got extinct?
(a) Lion (*Panthera leo*) (b) Panther (*Panthera pardus*) (c) Lynx (*Felis lynx*) (d) Cheetah (*Acinonyx jubatus*)

294. In the Trans-Himalayan biogeographical zone Hemis, Siachen Shyok and Rupshu protected areas are meant for an indicator species of carnivora. Name this species:
(a) Snow Leopard (*Panthera uncia*)
(b) Clouded Leopard (*Neofelis nebulosa*)
(c) Marbled Cat (*Felis marmorata*) (d) Leopard Cat (*Felis bengalensis*)

295. In which year was the International Snow Leopard Symposium held?
(a) 1986   (b) 1982   (c) 1960   (d) 1990

296. In some high rainfall zones (Western Ghats, North-Eastern India) there are black leopards. What is the phenomenon of blackening of coat colour called?
(a) Melanism   (b) Albinism (c) Colour defect   (d) None of the above

297. It is said that Panther (*Panthera pardus*) migrated into India before the Tiger (*Panthera tigris*) and before Sri Lanka separated from the main peninsula of India. What is the evidence?
(a) Panthers not found in Sri Lanka
(b) Tigers not found in Sri Lanka
(c) Panthers occur in Sri Lanka (d) (b) & (c) both

298. What is the name given to offspring produced by cross-breeding of Lion and Tigress?
(a) Liger   (b) Tigon
(c) Liontig   (d) Tiglion

299. What is the name given to an offspring produced by cross-breeding a Tiger and Lioness?
(a) Liger (b) Tigon (c) Liontig   (d) Tiglion

300. What is the cross between Tigon and Lion called?
(a) Litigon   (b) Tiglon (c) Ligeron   (d)   No term

301. Which is the smallest wild cat of India?
(a) Marbled Cat (*Felis marmorata*) (b) Golden Cat (*Felis temmincki*)   (c) Leopard Cat (*Felis bengalensis*) (d) Rustyspotted Cat (*Felis rubiginosa*)

302. To which family does the Lynx belong?
(a) Cat (b) Deer (c) Bird   (d) Antelope

303. Name the cat that appears to be a miniature Clouded Leopard. It occurs in NE India and feeds on birds and small mammals:

(a) Fishing Cat (*Felis viverrina*) (b) Desert Cat (*Felis libyca*) (c) Caracal (*Felis caracal*) (d) Marbled Cat (*Felis marmorata charltoni*)

304. Which cat looks like a miniature panther?
(a) Leopard Cat (*Felis bengalensis*) (b) Caracal (*Felis caracal*) (c) Lynx (*Felis lynx*) (d) None

305. Where does Pallas's Cat occur in India?
(a) Ladakh & Tibet (b) U.P. (c) M.P. (d) Kerala

306. Where does Lynx occur in India?
(a) Ladakh & Tibet (b) MP (c) Kerala (d) Maharashtra

307. Which animal shams dead when attacked by wild dogs (*Cuon alpinus*)?
(a) Striped Hyena (*Hyaena hyaena*) (b) Tiger (*Panthera tigris*) (c) Cheetal (*Axis axis*) (d) Hog Deer (*Axis porcinus*)

308. What is the litter size of a Clouded Leopard (*Neofelis nubulosa*)?
(a) 2 (b) 4 (c) 6 (d) 5

309. What is the litter size of an Ounce (*Panthera uncia*)?
(a) 2 to 4 (b) 1 to 2 (c) 1 (d) 6

310. What is the other name of the Ounce?
(a) Snow Leopard (b) Hunting Leopard (c) Leopard (d) Lynx

311. What is the other name of the Hunting Leopard?
(a) Cheetah (b) Black Panther (c) Snow Leopard (d) Lion

312. What is the gestation period of the Leopard (*Panthera pardus*)?

(a) 87 to 94 days (b) 100 to 120 days (c) 30 to 40 days (d) 50 to 60 days

313. What are the young ones of a cat called?
(a) Kitten (b) Chicken (c) Calf (d) Pup

314. What are the new-born of a Tiger called?
(a) Cub (b) Pup (c) Calf (d) Kitten

315. Name a mammal that thrives on carion and carcass of animals. It is represented by a single species in the family in India. However, 5 fossil species have been identified in the Siwalik deposits:
(a) Striped Hyena (*Hyaena hyaena*) (b) Tiger (*Panthera tigris*) (c) Chausingha (*Tetraceros guadricornis*) (d) None of the above

316. If W is the dominant gene for yellow coat colour and w is the recessive gene for coat colour, then what is the genetic make-up of the white tigers in India?
(a) WW (b) Ww (c) ww (d) W_2

317. What is the method applied for the Tiger census?
(a) Facemark Census (b) Pugmark Census (c) Direct Visual Count (d) Transect Sampling

318. In which realm you find the maximum number of species of Civets?
(a) Indo-Malayan Realm (b) Palearctic Realm (c) Afrotropical Realm (d) Oceanian Realm

319. From which species of Civet, the secretion of the scent glands is collected?

(a) Large Indian Civet (*Viverra zibetha*) (b) Small Indian Civet (*V. India*) (c) Tiger Civet (*Prionodon pardicolor*) (d) (a) & (b) both

320. What is a Tiger-Civet?
(a) Spotted Linsang (*Prionodon pardicolor*)
(b) Toddy Cat (*Paradoxurus hermaphroditus*)
(c) Bear Cat (*Arctictis binturong*) (d) None of the above

321. In Andaman & Nicobar Islands, a civet was introduced which became a serious pest of poultry and crops like banana (*Musa sp.*), coffee (*Coffea sp.*) and coconut (*Cocos nucifera*). Name the civet:
(a) Palm Civet (*Paradoxurus hermaphroditus*)
(b) Himalayan Palm Civet (*Paguma larvata*)
(c) Brown Palm Civet (*Parodoxurus jerdoni*)
(d) Bear Cat (*Arctiatis binturong*)

322. Which is the smallest civet in India?
(a) Spotted Linsang (*Prionodon pardicolor*)
(b) Toddy Cat   (c) Palm Civet (d) Bear Cat

323. To which group of animals are civets most closely related?
(a) Cat (b) Deer (c) Mongoose (d) Bears

324. What is the more popular name of the Binturong?
(a) Bear Cat   (b) Toddy Cat   (c) Tiger Cat
(d) Palm Civet

325. What is the distribution of the Binturong (*Arctictis binturong*)?
(a) Nepal & NE India (b) Rajasthan
(c) Kerala   (d) Madhya Pradesh

326. What kind of habitat does Binturong (*Arctictis binturong*) prefer?

(a) Dense forests   (b) Swamps   (c) Deserts
(d) Snows

327.   Which is the biggest civet in India?
       (a) Large Indian Civet (*Viverra zibetha*)
       (b) Himalayan Palm Civet (*Paguma larvata*)
       (c) Toddy Cat (*Paradoxurus hermaphroditus*)
       (d) None of the above

328.   Which civet in India has adapted to raid the containers in which villagers collect a drink from palm?
       (a) Toddy Cat (*Paradoxurus hermaphroditus*)
       (b) Tiger Civet (*Prionodon pardicolor*)
       (c) (a) & (b) both (d) None of the above

329.   Which species of civet in south India is currently facing extinction?
       (a) Malabar Civet (*Viverra megaspila*) (b) Small Indian Civet (*Viverricula indica*) (c) Large Indian Civet (*Viverra zibetha*) (d) None of the above

330.   How will you distinguish a civet from a mongoose?
       (a) Mongoose have comparatively large ears
       (b) Civets have comparatively large ears
       (c) Mongoose have perfume glands (d) Civets do not have scent glands.

331.   How is the Spotted Linsang different from other civets?
       (a) Absence of scent glands in Linsang
       (b) Presence of scent glands in Linsang
       (c) Linsang is a carnivore (d) No difference

332.   Which continent is supposed to be the place of origin of the Mongooses (*herpestidae*)
       (a) Africa   (b) Asia

(c) North America   (d) Australia

333. The Ruddy Mongoose (*Herpestes smithi*) has a peculiar method of procuring food; what is it?
(a) It smashes the shells of large snails against stones   (b) It steals flesh (c) It eats sand alongwith flesh (d) None of the above

334. Which is the largest mongoose in India?
(a) Stripednecked Mongoose (*Herpestes vitticollis*) (b) Crabeating Mongoose (*H. urva*) (c) Common Mongoose (*H. hardwicki*) (d) Ruddy Mongoose (*H. smithi*)

335. How many species of Mongoose are found in India?
(a) 5   (b) 6   (c) 7   (d) 8

336. Though all mongooses possess stink glands, only two Indian mongooses can use it in self-defence. Name them:
(a) Crabeating Mongoose (*Herpestes urva*) and Stripednecked Mongoose (*H. vitticollis*) (b) Common Mongoose (*H. edwardsi*) and Brown Mongoose (*H. fuscus*) (c) Crabeating Mongoose and Common Mongoose (d) Stripednecked and Brown Mongoose

337. Which animal is supposed to be ancestor of the domestic dog?
(a) Wolf (*Canis lupus*) (b) Wild Dog (*Cuon alpinus*) (c) Jackal (*Canis aureus*) (d) Red Fox (*Vulpes vulpes*)

338. Which animal is known as the whistling hunter?

(a) Wild dog (*Cuon alpinus*) (b) Tiger (*Panthera tigris*) (c) Lion (*Panthera leo*) (d) None of the above

339. What is the gestation period of the Dhole (*Cuon alpinus*)?
(a) 70 days (b) 100 days (c) 110 days (d) 120 days

340. What is the gestation period of the Red Fox (*Vulpes vulpes*)?
(a) 51-53 days (b) 61-63 days (c) 71-73 days (d) 81-83 days

341. Which animal hunts in packs?
(a) Dhole (*Cuon alpinus*) (b) Tiger (*Panthera tigris*) (c) Lion (*Panthera leo*) (d) Cheetal (*Axis axis*)

342. What is the young one of a wolf called?
(a) Whelp (b) Kitten (c) Cub (d) Pup

343. To which family does the wolf (*Canis lupus*) belong?
(a) Dog (b) Cat (c) Weasel (d) Rodent

344. What is the young one of a Red Fox (*Vulpes vulpes*) called?
(a) Cub (b) Pup (c) Vixen (d) Doe

345. Which of the following animals shams dead when under severe threat of being attacked?
(a) Indian Fox (*Vulpes bengalensis*) (b) Hyena (*Hyaena hyeana*) (c) Jackal (*Canis aureus*) (d) All above

346. Is Red Panda (*Ailurus fulgens*) found in India?
(a) Yes (b) No

347. Is Giant Panda (*Ailuropoda melanoleuca*) found within Indian limits?
(a) Yes (b) No (c) So far not recorded

348. What is the more popular name of the Red Panda (*Ailurus fulgens*)?
(a) Cat Bear (b) Rat Bear (c) Weasel (d) Black Bear

349. Which animal in India has the thick hairy soles?
(a) Red Panda (*Ailurus fulgens*) (b) Giant Panda (*Ailuropoda melanoleuca*) (c) Ratel (*Mellivora capensis*) (d) Marbled Polecat (*Vormela peregusna*)

350. Is Red Panda primarily a herbivore?
(a) Yes (b) No

351. Where is the Red Panda (*Ailurus fulgens*) found in India?
(a) Sikkim (b) Andhra Pradesh (c) Rajasthan (d) Kerala

352. Which animal is adapted to gather food by breaking down the termite mond and then apply suction?
(a) Sloth Bear (*Melursus ursinus*) (b) Indian Hare (*Lepus nigricollis*) (c) Painted Bat (*Kerivoula picta*) (d) Common Mongoose (*Herpestes edwardsi*)

353. What is the common food of a Sloth Bear (*Melursus ursinus*)?
(a) Termites (b) Herbs (c) Fruits (d) (a) & (c) both

354. What is the new-born of the bear called?
(a) Cub (b) Fawn (c) Calf (d) Leveret

355. What is the condition of a new-born bear cub?

(a) Hairless and blind   (b) Hairy and blind (c) Hairy and open-eyed (d) None of the above

356. How long does a bear cub remain blind after birth?
(a) 4 months   (b) 1 month   (c) 10 days (d) 40 days

357. What is the colour of claws of the Sloth Bear (*Melursus ursinus*)?
(a) Black   (b) Red   (c) White   (d) Grey

358. What is the habitat distribution of the Sloth Bear in India?
(a) North-East   (b) Deccan Peninsula (c) Whole of India from Himalayan foothills (d) None of the above

359. Name a bear with brown coat living in the Western Himalaya:
(a) Brown Bear (*Ursus arctos*) (b) Himalayan Black Bear (*Selenarctos thibetanus*) (c) Sloth Bear (*Melursus ursinus*) (d) Malayan Sun Bear (*Helarctos malayanus*)

360. Carnivora is a very diverse order of mammals. Alaskan sub-species of one bear is the largest living carnivore with adults measuring up to 280 cm in body length and weighing up to 780 kg. Name the species:
(a) Brown Bear (*Ursus arctos*) (b) Himalayan Black Bear (*Selenarctos thibetanus*) (c) Sloth Bear (*Melursus ursinus*) (d) Malayan Sun Bear (*Helarctos malayanus*)

361. Name the rarest bear in the world?
(a) Asiatic Black Bear (*Selenarctos thibetanus*) (b) Malayan Sun Bear (*Helarctos malayanus*)

(c) Sloth Bear (*Melursus ursinus*) (d) None of the above

362. What is the habitat distribution of the Malayan Sun Bear (*Helarctos malayanus*)
     (a) North-east India   (b) Deccan Peninsula
     (c) Ceylon   (d) Western India

363. How many species of bear are found in India?
     (a) 4   (b) 5   (c) 6   (d) 7

364. Which is the smallest bear in India?
     (a) Sloth Bear (*Melursus ursinus*)
     (b) Malayan Sun Bear (*Helarctos malayanus*)
     (c) Black Bear (*Selenarctos thibetanus*)

365. Does Brown Bear bury itself under the snow to pass the winters in torpid sleep?
     (a) Yes   (b) No

366. Does Sloth Bear in India bury itself under the snow to pass the winter in torpid sleep?
     (a) Yes (b) No

367. Is Brown Bear the highest altitude living bear of India?
     (a) Yes (b) No

368. Does the female Brown Bear give birth to cubs during its winter hibernation?
     (a) Yes (b) No

369. Is Otter primarily an aquatic mammal?
     (a) Yes (b) No

370. Are Martens, Weasels and Polecats terrestrial and arboreal animals?
     (a) Yes (b) No

371. Which species is the smallest among the Indian Otters?

(a) Clawless Otter (*Aonyx cinerea*)
(b) Common Otter (*Lutra lutra*) (c) Smooth Indian Otter (*Lutra perspicillata*) (d) Difficult to say

372. How many species of Otters are found in India?
(a) 3   (b) 4   (c) 5   (d) 6

373. Is it true that Otters are not found in Australia, New Zealand and Poles?
(a) Yes (b) No

374. Which animal in India is known as Water Dog (*Pani ka Kutta*)?
(a) Blue Whale (*Balaenoptera musculus*)
(b) Smooth Indian Otter (*Lutra perspicillata*)
(c) Sperm Whale (*Physeter catodon*)
(d) Common Dolphin (*Delphinus delphis*)

375. Name the only Weasel in India that changes its brown summer coat to a snow-white coat during the snowy winters of the Himalaya:
(a) Stoat (*Mustela erminea*) (b) Pale Weasel (*M. altaica*) (c) Yellowbellied Weasel (*M. kathiah*) (d) No such species found in India

376. Is it true that Weasels living in the high Himalaya have hairy soles?
(a) Yes (b) No

377. What is the main food of the Otters?
(a) Fish (b) Birds (c) Fruits (d) Carion

378. What is the period of gestation in the Otters?
(a) 50 days (b) 60 days (c) 70 days (d) 80 days

379. Which species of Otter is kept as pet by fishermen to facilitate the fish capture?
(a) *Lutra perspiciliata* (b) *Lutra lutra* (c) *Anoyx cinerea* (d) No such practice prevails in India

380. How many species of Martens are found in India?
    (a) 1 (b) 2 (c) 3 (d) 4
381. Which is the largest Marten in India?
    (a) Yellow-throated Marten (*Martes flavigula*)
    (b) Stone Marten (*Martes foina*)
382. Name a high-altitude mammal which looks like a cat and squirrel:
    (a) Stone Marten (*Martes foina*) (b) Serotine (*Eptesicus serotinus*) (c) Clawless Otter (*Aonyx cinerea*) (d) Kashmir Flying Squirrel (*Hylopetes fimbriatus*)
383. What is the food of a Weasel?
    (a) Rat, mice and birds (b) Fruits and grasses (c) Mahua flowers (d) Omnivorous habit
384. In India only two species of Ferret-Badgers are found. Name the species:
    (a) *Melogale moschata and M. personata* (b) *Martes flavigula and M. foina* (c) *Axis axis and A. porcinus* (d) *Panthera tigris and P. pardus*
385. Name an animal having bear-like body with pale white above and black on the side and below:
    (a) Honey Badger (*Mellivora capensis*)
    (b) Chinese Ferret Badger (*Melogale moschata*)
    (c) Hog Badger (*Arctonyx collaris*) (d) Burmese Ferret Badger (*Melogale personata*)
386. Are true Badgers found in India?
    (a) Yes (b) No
387. To which natural order tree shrews, hedgehogs and moles belong?
    (a) Carnivora (b) Insectivora (c) Rodentia (d) Artiodactyla

388. What is a Tupaia?
    (a) Tree Shrew (b) Hedgehog (c) Mole
    (d) Ground Shrew
389. What is the primary food of the Indian Tree
    Shrew (*Anathana ellioti*)?
    (a) Insects (b) Tree roots (c) Grass (d) Not
    known
390. Which animal has remarkable ability to
    stretch its body skin to cover head and limbs
    and role up into spiky ball?
    (a) Indian Tree Shrew (*Anathana ellioti*)
    (b) Eastern Mole (*Talpa mucrura*)
    (c) Longeared Hedgehog (*Hemiechinus
    auritus*) (d) Grey Musk Shrew (*Suncus
    murinus*)
391. What is the popular name of the Grey Musk
    Shrew (*Suncus murinus*)?
    (a) Rat (b) Musk Rat (c) Painted Bat
    (d) Ground Rat
392. Which is the only mammal with wings?
    (a) Bat (*Chiroptera*) (b) Tupaia (*Insectivora*)
    (c) Weasel (*Mustelidae*) (d) Cheetal
    (*Artiodactyla*)
393. Is Flying Fox (*Pteropus giganteus*) the largest
    Indian bat?
    (a) Yes (b) No
394. Is Flying Fox (*Pteropus giganteus*) a true fox?
    (a) Yes (b) No
395. Is it true that only one species of bat, the
    Serotine (*Eptesicus serotinus*) is found in both
    the eastern and western hemispheres?
    (a) Yes (b) No
396. Is *Latidens salimali* the rarest bat in India?

(a) Yes (b) No

397. What is the food of the Flying Fox (*Pteropus giganteus*)?
(a) Fruit juice (b) Insects (c) Roots (d) Leaves

398. What is the gestation period of the Flying Fox (*Pteropus giganteus*)?
(a) 145 days (b) 165 days (c) 175 days (d) 190 days

399. Does Fulvous Fruit Bat (*Rousettus leschenaulti*) have large and brilliant eyes?
(a) Yes (b) No

400. What is main food of the Indian false Vampire (*Megaderma lyra*)?
(a) Insects (b) Fruits (c) Leaves (d) Roots

401. Does Indian false Vampire (*Megaderma lyra*) belong to bat family?
(a) Yes (b) No

402. To which group does Serotine (*Eptesicus serotinus*) belong?
(a) Cat (b) Rat (c) Bat (d) Voles

403. To which group does Indian Pipistrelle, (*Pipistrellus coromandra*) belong?
(a) Cat (b) Rat (c) Bat (d) Voles

404. Name a bat with bright orange coloured body and black wings?
(a) Bearded Sheathtailed Bat (*Taphozous melanopogon*) (b) Painted Bat (*Kerivoula picta*) (c) Shortnosed Fruit Bat (*Cynopterus sphinx*) (d) Tickell's Bat (*Hesperopterus tickelli*)

405. Name a Flying Squirrel found in the higher Himalaya?
(a) Kashmir, Woolly Flying Squirrel (*Eupetaurus cinereus*) (b) Hodgsons' Flying

Squirrel (*Petaurista magnificus*)
(c) Particoloured Flying Squirrel (*Hylopetes alboniger*) (d) Common Giant Flying Squirrel (*Petaurista petaurista*)

406. What is the movement of Flying Squirrel called?
(a) Flying (b) Gliding (c) Crawling
(d) Creeping

407. What device helps the Flying Squirrels in gliding?
(a) Feathers (b) Extended skin membrane
(c) Wings (d) No special device

408. Can Flying Squirrel sustain its aerial movement by wing beats?
(a) Yes (b) No

409. Name the squirrel having five pale stripes on its back?
(a) Five Striped Palm Squirrel (*Funambulus penanti*) (b) Three Striped Palm Squirrel (*F. palmarum*) (c) Dusky Striped Squirrel (*F. sublineatus*) (d) Himalayan Striped Squirrel (*Callosciurus macclellandi*)

410. To which group Marmots belong?
(a) Cats (b) Squirrel (c) Dogs (d) Bats

411. What is the range of distribution of Marmots in India?
(a) Higher Himalayas (b) Deccan Peninsula
(c) Western Ghats (d) Eastern Ghats

412. Where do the Marmots live?
(a) Burrow in the ground (b) Grass nest on trees (c) Water streams (d) No specific haunt

413. What is the popular name of the Gerbilles?

(a) Tiger Civet (b) Marmots (c) Antelope Rats (d) Bear Cat

414. How you will distinguish a rat from a Gerbille?
(a) Rats have hairy tail (b) Gerbilles have hairy tail (c) Rats live in burrows (d) Gerbilles live on trees

415. What are the exit holes of the rats' burrow called?
(a) Bolt holes (b) Escape holes (c) Escape routes (d) Jolt holes

416. To which family does the Metad (*Millardia meltada*) belong?
(a) Rat (b) Cat (c) Bat (d) None of the above

417. What is the zoological name of the common House Rat?
(a) *Rattus rattus* (b) *Bandicota indica* (c) *Rattus norvegicus* (d) *Mus musculus*

418. How many species of the Bamboo Rats are found in India?
(a) 2 (b) 4 (c) 6 (d) 8

419. What is the peculiarity of the Indian Porcupine (*Hystrix indica*)?
(a) Hairs modified into spines (b) Hairs modified into scales (c) Hairs modified into wings (d) No peculiarity

420. What are the modified hairs in the Indian Porcupine called?
(a) Quills (b) Feathers (c) Thorns (d) Blades

421. Is Indian Porcupine (*Hystrix indica*) a burrow dweller?
(a) Yes (b) No

422. What is the main food of the Porcupines?

(a) Vegetables and grains (b) Insects (c) **Birds** (d) Mammals

423. Which species of Porcupine has tuft of bristle at the tip of the tail?

(a) Brushtailed Porcupine (*Atherurus macrourus*) (b) Hodgsons' Porcupine (*Hystrix hodgsoni*) (c) Indian Porcupine (*Hystrix indica*) (d) None of the above

424. Does true Rabbit exist in India ?

(a) Yes (b) No

425. True Rabbits are not found in India but a nearest relative is found in the Himalayan foothills. Name this species:

(a) Indian Hare (*Lepus nigricollis*) (b) Himalayan Mouse Hare (*Ochotona roylei*) (c) Hispid Hare (*Caprolagus hispidus*) (d) No nearest relative found in India

426. Name the hare having coarse fur of dark brown bristles?

(a) Hispid Hare (*Caprolagus hispidus*) (b) Indian Hare (*Lepus nigricollis*) (c) Himalayan Mouse Hare (*Ochotona roylei*) (d) No such species exists

427. Is Assam Rabbit a true rabbit?

(a) Yes (b) No

428. Is Assam Rabbit and Hispid Hare synonyms?

(a) Yes (b) No

429. Which is the largest land mammal in India?

(a) Indian Onehorned Rhinoceros (*Rhinoceros unicornis*) (b) Indian Elephant (*Elephas maximus*) (c) Asiatic Wild Ass (*Equus hemionus*)

430. Which animal has the longest gestation period?
(a) Elephant (b) Gaur (c) Wild Ass (d) Rhinoceros

431. What is the male elephant called?
(a) Bull (b) Hind (c) Gander (d) Buck

432. What is the young one of an Elephant called?
(a) Calf (b) Fawn (c) Leveret (d) Pup

433. What is the elephant's tusk?
(a) Modified incisor (b) Modified molar (c) Modified premolar (d) Special teeth

434. What kind of teeth are the tusks of the Indian Elephant (*Elephas maximus*)?
(a) Second pair of incisor in the upper jaw
(b) Second pair of incisor in the lower jaw
(c) First pair of incisor in the upper jaw
(d) First pair of incisor in the lower jaw

435. What is the name given to a male elephant without tusk?
(a) Makna (b) Makra (c) Ganesha (d) Rogue

436. What is the Indian name for an elephant with one tusk?
(a) Makna (b) Makra (c) Ganesha (d) Rogue

437. Maknas and cow elephants do not possess tusks but have short protrusions. What are these protrusions called?
(a) Tufts (b) Teeth (c) Tushes (d) Tusks

438. The longest recorded tusk from the African Elephant (*Loxodonta africana*) is 336 cm. What is the length of the longest recorded tusk from Indian Elephant (*Elephas maximus*)?
(a) 299 cm (b) 301 cm (c) 305 cm (d) 306 cm

439. Is *Stegodon ganesa* an extinct elephant-like animal from India?
(a) Yes (b) No

440. Is Indian Elephant (*Elephas maximus*) larger than the African Elephant (*Loxodonta africana*)?
(a) Yes (b) No

441. Is it true that the trunk of the Indian Elephant has single lip whereas the African Elephant has two equal lips?
(a) Yes (b) No

442. How many nails does Indian Elephant possess on the hindfoot?
(a) 4 (b) 5 (c) 6 (d) No nails

443. How many nails does African Elephant possess on the hindfoot?
(a) 3 (b) 4 (c) 5 (d) No nails

444. What is the gestation period of the Indian Elephant (*Elephas maximus*)?
(a) 18 months (b) 22 months (c) 24 months (d) 30 months

445. Normally, how many calves are born to an Indian Elephant (*Elephas maximus*)?
(a) 1 (b) 3 (c) 4 (d) 5

446. Do elephants have poor sight?
(a) Yes (b) No

447. Do elephants have least developed sense of hearing?
(a) Yes (b) No

448. Do elephants have highly developed sense of smell?
(a) Yes (b) No

449. What is a Pachyderm?
(a) Elephant (b) Sambhar (c) Snake (d) Gaur

450. How many species of living Rhinoceros are found in India?
(a) 1 (b) 2 (c) 3 (d) 4

451. There are five species of Rhinos in the world—two in Africa and three in Asia. African Rhinos-Black Rhino (*Diceros bicornis*) and White Rhino (*Ceratotherium simum*) have two long horns. In Asia Javan Rhino (*Rhinoceros sondiacus*) and Indian Rhino (*R. unicornis*) have a single horn. Name the third Asian species having two smaller horns:
(a) Sumatran Rhino (*Didermocerus sumatrensis*)
(b) Asiatic two-horned Rhino (c) (a) & (b) are synonyms

452. Which is the second largest land mammal in India?
(a) Indian Onehorned Rhinoceros (*Rhinoceros unicornis*) (b) Sumatran Rhino (*Didermocerus sumatrensis*) (c) Indian Elephant (*Elephas maximus*) (d) Gaur (*Bos gaurus*)

453. Until the end of 19th century which living species of Rhino existed in India?
(a) Sumatran Rhino (*Didermocerus sumatrensis*)
(b) Javan Rhino (*Rhinoceros sondiacus*) (c) (a) & (b) both (d) None of the above

454. What is the age of sexual maturity in Indian Rhinoceros (*Rhinoceros unicornis*)?
(a) Male 3 years, female 5 years (b) Male 10 years, female 5 years (c) Male 13 years, female 7 years (d) Not known

455. What is the new-born of a Rhino called?

(a) Calf (b) Cygnet (c) Gosling (d) Piglet

456. What is the approximate weight of the new-born calf of the Indian Rhinoceros (*Rhinoceros unicornis*)?
(a) 30 kg (b) 40 kg (c) 50 kg (d) 60 kg

457. What is the approximate weight of the adult Indian Rhinoceros (*R. unicornis*)?
(a) 800 kg (b) 1000 kg (c) 1820 kg (d) 1920 kg

458. Indian Rhino has been slaughtered for its horn which fetches mind-boggling price in the international market. What is the approximate value of Rhino horn per kg?
(a) 20,000 U.S. dollars (b) 30,000 U.S. dollars (c) 40,000 U.S. dollars (d) 50,000 U.S. dollars

459. What is the alleged medicinal property of Rhino horn?
(a) Diuretic (b) Aphrodisiac (c) Blood Purifier (d) Laxative

460. Has Javan Rhinoceros (*Rhinoceros sondiacus*), which lived in Bengal and North-east, become extinct in India?
(a) Yes (b) No

461. Is Asiatic Two-horned Rhinoceros (*Didermocerus sumatrensis*) now extinct in India?
(a) Yes (b) No

462. There are 5 species of Rhinos living in the world. As per body size gradation what is the position of the Indian Onehorned Rhino (*Rhinoceros unicornis*) in the world?
(a) Largest (b) Second largest (c) Third largest (d) Smallest

463. Name one species of fossil Rhino found in the Siwalik beds:
   (a) *Rhinoceros sivalensis* (b) *R. sondiacus* (c) *R. unicornis* (d) *Diceros bicornis*

464. Name the species found in the Little Runn of Kutch where it occupies the grassy habitat islands called *bets:*
   (a) Indian Wild Ass (*Asinus hemionus*) (b) Cheetal (*Axis axis*) (c) Blue Whale (*Balaenoptera musculus*) (d) Hog Deer (*Axis porcinus*)

465. Which is the largest Wild Ass of India?
   (a) Indian Wild Ass (*Asinus hemionus*) (b) Tibetan Wild Ass (*Asinus kiang*)

466. How many species of Wild Ass are found in India?
   (a) 2   (b) 4   (c) 6   (d) 8

467. Name the largest mammal of the Indian hot deserts:
   (a) Indian Wild Ass (*Asinus hemionus*) (b) Gaur (*Bos gaurus*) (c) Indian Elephant (*Elephas maximus*) (d) Sambhar (*Cervus unicolor*)

468. Name the country which possesses the maximum number of Cervids in the world?
   (a) Nepal (b) India (c) Bhutan (d) Pakistan

469. Which Deer has the widest distribution in the world?
   (a) Sambhar (*Cervus unicolor*) (b) Cheetal (*Axis axis*) (c) Hog Deer (*Axis porcinus*) (d) Muntjak (*Muntiacus muntjak*)

470. Which is the tallest of all surviving Wild Oxen in the world?

(a) Gaur (*Bos gaurus*)   (b) Yak (*Bos grunnies*)
(c) Banteng (*Bos banteng*)   (d) Wild Buffalo
(*Bubalus bubalis*)

471. Which is the least endangered Wild Bovine in Asia?
(a) Gaur (*Bos gaurus*)   (b) Yak (*Bos grunnies*)
(c) Banteng (*Bos banteng*)   (d) Wild Buffalo
(*Bubalus bubalis*)

472. Which animal in India has the longest horns of any living wild animal in the world?
(a) Asiatic Wild Buffalo (*Bubalus bubalis*) (b) Gaur (*Bos gaurus*)   (c) Sambhar (*Cervus unicolor*)   (d) Banteng (*Bos banteng*)

473. What is the popular name of the Gaur (*Bos gaurus*)?
(a) Indian Bison (b) Wild Buffalo (c) Tsaine (d) Musk Ox

474. What is the probable distribution of the Banteng (*Bos banteng*) within Indian limits?
(a) Manipur   (b) Assam   (c) Kerala
(d) Andaman & Nicobar Islands

475. What is the other name of the Banteng?
(a) Tsaine (b) Bharal (c) Goral (d) Nayan

476. What is the distribution of Yak (*Bos grunnies*) within India?
(a) Changechenmo Valley, Ladakh
(b) Manipur (c) Tripura (d) Madhya Pradesh

477. Is it true that Asiatic Wild Buffalo (*Bubalus bubalis*) is one of the most important wild genetic resources which has the potential for disease-resistant breeding in the domestic buffalo stock?
(a) Yes (b) No

478. Have rinderpest and foot-and-mouth diseases decimated the population of Gaur (*Bos gaurus*) in India?
(a) Yes (b) No

479. What is Nayan (*Ovis ammon*) otherwise known as?
(a) Great Tibetan Sheep (b) Marco Polo's Sheep (c) Blue Sheep (d) Wild Sheep

480. What is the Shapu (*Ovis orientalis*)?
(a) Wild Sheep (b) Wild Goat (c) Antelope (d) Wild Oxen

481. Name the only place in India where Marco Polo's Sheep (*Ovis ammon poliy*) exist:
(a) Hunza (b) Garhwal (c) Kumaon (d) Pamirs

482. Name the animal which is supposedly the ancestor of domestic sheep stock:
(a) Urial (b) Red Sheep (*Ovis Orientalis*) (c) (a) & (b) are synonyms (d) Not known

483. Which animal morphologically holds the place between sheep and goat?
(a) Bharal (*Pseudois nayaur*) (b) Ibex (*Capra ibex*) (c) Markhor (*Capra falconeri*) (d) Takin (*Budorcas taxicolor*)

484. There are three species of animals in India which are neither goat nor antelope but possess certain characteristics of both. Two species are the Serrow (*Capricornis sumatrensis*) and Goral (*Nemorhaedus goral*). Which is the third one?
(a) Muntjak (*Muntiacus muntjak*) (b) Takin (*Budorcas taxicolor*) (c) Chiru (*Pantholops hodgsoni*) (d) No such animal exists

485. Which animal in India is a relative of the Saiga Antelope of Russia?
(a) Chiru or Tibetan Antelope   (b) Takin
(c) Serrow (d) Tahr

486. Which is the only Wild Goat found in South India?
(a) Nilgiri Tahr (*Hemitragus hylocrius*)
(b) Serrow (*Capricornis sumatrensis*) (c) Chiru (*Pantholops hodgsoni*) (d) Takin (*Budorcas taxicolor*)

487. Does Chiru (*Pantholops hodgsoni*) have the peculiar swollen nose?
(a) Yes (b) No

488. Which antelope in India possesses the remarkably swollen nose?
(a) Tibetan Antelope (*Pantholops hodgsoni*)
(b) Fourhorned Antelope (*Tetracerus quadricornis*) (c) Indian Antelope (*Antilope cervicapra*) (d) Nilgai (*Boselaphus tragocamelus*)

489. How is Indian Gazelle (*Gazella gazella*) popularly known?
(a) Chinkara (b) Thamin (c) Nilgai
(d) Pangolin

490. How is the Tibetan Gazelle scientifically known?
(a) *Procapia picticaudata* (b) *Gazella gazella*
(c) *Cervus eldi* (d) *Axis axis*

491. Which is the largest Asian Antelope?
(a) Nilgai (*Boselaphus tragocamelus*)
(b) Chausingha (*Tetracerus quadricornis*)
(c) Black Buck (*Antilope cervicapra*) (d) Chiru (*Pantholops hodgsoni*)

492. Name the only animal with four horns:

(a) Nilgai (*Boselaphus tragocamelus*)
(b) Chausingha (*Tetracerus quadricornis*)
(c) Black Buck (*Antilope cervicapra*) (d) Chiru
(*Pantholops hodgsoni*)

493. What is the *Sivathericum*?
(a) A fossil ruminant found in Siwalik beds
(b) Largest known ruminant to have existed on earth (c) A fossil ruminant with four horns (d) All above are correct

494. What is the difference between Gazelle and Antelope?
(a) Gazelles have tufts of hair on the knees
(b) In the Gazelles horns appear in both sexes (c) Horns of the Gazelle are ringed throughout the length (d) All above

495. Is it true that antlers (horns) of the Deer are not twisted as in the case of horns of sheep and goats?
(a) Yes (b) No

496. Is it true that Deer shed and regain their antlers periodically?
(a) Yes (b) No

497. Is it true that unlike the solid antlers of Deer, Oxen have the hollow horns with a bony case?
(a) Yes (b) No

498. Is it true that in the Bovidae (oxen, sheep and goats) horns does not persist throughout the life?
(a) Yes (b) No

499. Which species of Deer found in Manipur is currently the most endangered wild mammal in Asia?

(a) Browantlered Deer (*Cervus eldi eldi*)
(b) Musk Deer (*Moschus moschiferus*) (c) Indian Chevrotain (*Tragulus meminna*) (d) Muntjak (*Muntiacus muntjak*)

500. What is the popular name of the Browantlered Deer (*Cervus eldi eldi*) in Manipur?
(a) Sangai (b) Hangul (c) Sambhar (d) Cheetal

501. What is the current population of the Sangai deer in the wild?
(a) Less than 50 (b) More than 200 (c) More than 300 (d) More than 400

502. What is the natural predator of the Sangai?
(a) Tiger (*Panthera tigris*) (b) Lion (*Panthera leo*) (c) Leopard (*Panthera pardus*) (d) No natural predator of Sangai

503. Name the smallest true deer of the Indian sub-continent:
(a) Indian Chevrotain (*Tragulus meminna*) (b) Muntjak (*Muntiacus muntjak*) (c) Hog Deer (*Axis porcinus*) (d) Sambhar (*Cervus unicolor*)

504. What is the female deer called?
(a) Buck (b) Doe (c) Sow (d) Cow

505. What is the male deer called?
(a) Buck (b) Doe (c) Sow (d) Bull

506. What is the young one of a deer called?
(a) Fawn (b) Calf (c) Pup (d) Cub

507. What is the young one of a hare called?
(a) Fawn (b) Leveret (c) Pup (d) Cub

508. The Kashmir Stag or the Hangul is a close relative of which of the following deer?

(a) The Red Deer (*Cervus elaphus*) (b) Sambar (*Cervus unicolor*) (c) Thamin (*Cervus eldi*) (d) None of the above

509. What is the current status of population of the Hangul (*Cervus elaphus hanglu*) in the wild?

(a) 500 (b) 600 (c) 700 (d) 800

510. Which deer in India has tusks?

(a) Musk Deer (*Moschus moschiferus*) (b) Mouse Deer (*Tragulus meminna*) (c) (a) & (b) both (d) No such deer exists

511. The Swamp Deer or Barasingha has two races in India. One—*Cervus duvauceli duvauceli*—found in the terai areas of U.P and Assam and two—*Cervus duvauceli branderi*—now confined to Kanha National Park of M.P. What is the difference between the two races?

(a) *C. d. duvauceli* has splayed hooves as it lives in swamps (b) *C. d. branderi* lives in hard ground, hence has well-knit hooves (c) *C. d. duvauceli* has larger skull (d) (a), (b) & (c) all are correct

512. Name this Deer which, interestingly, is absent in the Deccan Peninsula but occurs in Ceylon and low alluvial plains of north India and Assam. It is a close relative of Chital (*Axis axis*):

(a) Hog Deer (*Axis porcinus*) (b) Musk Deer (*Moschus moschiferus*) (c) Barking Deer (*Muntiacus muntjak*) (d) Swamp Deer (*Cervus duvauceli*)?

513. What is the term given to rutting call of a Barasingha Stag (*Cervus duvauceli*)?
(a) Cry (b) Bugle (c) Barking (d) Hissing

514. Which Deer in India is considered as undeveloped form of deer holding a morphological (structure) position between the Deer and the Antelope?
(a) Musk Deer (b) Barking Deer (c) Hog Deer (d) Spotted Deer

515. What is the peculiarity of a Musk Deer (*Moschus moschiferus*)?
(a) Antlers and face glands are wanting (b) Presence of Musk gland beneath the skin of abdomen (c) Presence of tusks (d) All above

516. Is musk gland found in the female Musk Deer?
(a) Yes (b) No

517. What is the habitat distribution of the Musk Deer (*Moschus moschiferus*)?
(a) Kashmir, Sikkim & Nepal (b) Deccan Peninsula (c) Central India (d) Ceylon

518. Name the only Deer which possesses tushes as well as antlers in India:
(a) Musk Deer (*Moschus moschiferus*) (b) Barking Deer (*Muntiacus muntjak*) (c) Para (*Axis porcinus*) (d) No such deer exists

519. How many pairs of teats does Pygmy Hog (*Sus salvanius*) possess?
(a) 3 (b) 4 (c) 5 (d) 6

520. How many species of Wild Pigs are found in India?
(a) 1   (b) 2   (c) 3   (d) 4

521. What is the female of a Pig called?
(a) Boar (b) Sow (c) Pen (d) Doe
522. What is the male of a Pig called?
(a) Boar (b) Sow (c) Pen (d) Doe
523. Which animal, believed to have been extinct, was discovered surviving along the foothills of Assam?
(a) Para (*Axis porcinus*) (b) Pygmy Hog (*Sus salvanius*) (c) Chiru *(Pantholops hodgsoni)* (d) Brown Bear (*Ursus arctos*)
524. What is the food of the Indian Pangolin (*Manis crassicaudata*) and the Chinese Pangolin (*M. pentadactyla*)?
(a) Termite, their eggs and ants (b) Fruits (c) Grass (d) Carion
525. Is Pangolin also known as scaly ant-eater?
(a) Yes (b) No
526. Which is the largest animal living today?
(a) Indian Elephant (*Elephas maximus*)
(b) Blue Whale (*Balaenoptera musculus*)
(c) Killer Whale (*Orcinus orca*) (d) Indian Rhinoceros (*Rhinoceros unicornis*)
527. What is the approximate weight of an adult Blue Whale (*Balaenoptera musculus*)?
(a) 50 tons (b) 100 tons (c) 150 tons (d) 200 tons
528. Name the largest of all toothed Whales in which female grows up to 50 feet in length:
(a) Sperm Whale (*Physeter macrocephalus*)
(b) Finner Whale (*Balaenoptera physalus*)
(c) Sei Whale (*B. borealis*) (d) Lesser Rorqual (*B. acutorostrata*)

529. Which is the largest living carnivore Whale capable of killing and tearing animals twice its own length?
(a) Killer Whale (*Orcinus orca*) (b) Sperm Whale (*Physeter catodon*) (c) Humpbacked Whale (*Megaptera novaeangliae*) (d) No such Whale exists

530. In the Indian subcontinent there are two species of Dolphins adapted to freshwater habitat. One is the Ganges Dolphin (*Platanista gangetica*) and the second :
(a) Common Dolphin (*Delphinus delphis*)
(b) Plumbeous Dolphin (*Sotalia plumbea*)
(c) Bottle-nosed Dolphin (*Tursiops aduncus*)
(d) Indus Dolphin (*Platanista indi*)

531. Which of the following animals have tusks?
(a) The Dugong (*Dugong dugon*) (b) Killer Whale (*Orcinus orca*) (c) Sperm Whale (*Physeter catodon*) (d) None of the above

532. What is the new-born of a Whale called?
(a) Calf (b) Fawn (c) Pup (d) Bull

533. What is the male Whale called?
(a) Bull (b) Cob (c) Buck (d) Male

7

THE BIRDS

534. Which is the national bird of India?
(a) Common Peafowl (*Pavo cristatus*) (b) Blyths' Baza (*Aviceda jerdoni*) (c) Great Indian

Bustard (*Choriotis nigriceps*) (d) Hooded Crane (*Grus monacha*)

535. The largest bird in the world living today—Ostrich—was found in India whose fossils were recovered and studied by a scientist, Lydekker. Name the hill ranges where the fossils were found:
(a) Western Ghats (b) Eastern Ghats (c) Siwalik & Himalayan Foothills (d) Aravallis

536. What is the range of the body temperature of the birds?
(a) 38° to 44°C (b) 44° to 50°C (c) 10° to 15°C (d) 20° to 30°C

537. Is normal body temperature of birds higher than the mammals?
(a) Yes (b) No

538. Air sacs are peculiar internal features of which group of animals?
(a) Mammals (b) Birds (c) Reptiles (d) Amphibians

539. Is sense of sight and hearing well developed in birds?
(a) Yes (b) No

540. Which is the fastest flying bird and in fact fastest flying creature in the world?
(a) Peregrine Falcon (*Falco peregrinus*) (b) Grey Shrike (*Lanius exubitor*) (c) Golden Eagle (*Aquila chrysaetos*) (d) Sooty Falcon (*Falco concolor*)

541. Which is the most aerial bird of India?

(a) Common Swift (*Apus apus*) (b) Stone Curlew (*Burhinus oedicnemus*) (c) Crab Plover (*Dromas ardeola*) (d) Rosy Pastor (*Sturnus roseus*)

542. Which is the most abundant domesticated bird in India?
(a) Crow (b) Parakeet (c) Chicken (d) Sparrow

543. Which group of birds have the most acute vision?
(a) Pheasants (b) Birds of Prey (*Falconiformes*) (c) Ducks (d) Cranes

544. What is the State bird of Andhra Pradesh?
(a) Indian Roller (*Coracias benghalensis*) (b) Sparrow (*Passer domesticus*) (c) Lapwing (*Vanellus vanellus*) (d) Dunlin (*Calidris alpina*)

545. There is only one family of bird in the world in which individuals hold food item in one foot and bite pieces off, as we eat a sandwich. Name this family:
(a) Psittacidae (*Parakeets*) (b) Laridae (*Gulls and Terns*) (c) Columbidae (*Pigeons & Doves*) (d) Strigidae (*Owls*)

546. Identify the bird making the largest nest in India:
(a) Megapode (*Megapodius freycinet*) (b) Violet Cuckoo (*Chalcites Xanthorhynchus*) (c) Black Stork (*Ciconia nigra*) (d) Painted Stork (*Mycteria leucocephala*)

547. What is the circumference of the nest of the Megapode (*Megapodius freycinet*)?
(a) 10m (b) 20m (c) 30m (d) 10 cm

548. Which Indian bird has the longest claws?

(a) Pheasant-tailed Jacana (*Hydrophasianus chirurgus*) (b) Bronze-winged Jacana (*Metopidius indicus*) (c) Avocet (*Recurvirostra avocetta*) (d) Corn Crake (*Crex crex*)

549. Which Indian bird has the shortest legs?
(a) Crested Tree Swift (*Hemiprocne longipennis*) (b) Palm Swift (*Cypsiurus parvus*) (c) Swift (*Apus apus*) (d) Alpine Swift (*Apus melba*)

550. Which is the highest altitude living bird?
(a) Yellow-billed or Alpine Chough (*Pyrrhocorax graculus*) (b) Red-billed Chough (*P. pyrrhocorax*) (c) Raven (*Corvus corax*) (d) Nutcracker (*Nucifraga caryocataractes*)

551. Of the 9,016 known species of the birds in the world, some 6000 species belong to the passeriformes order or completely terrestrial or arboreal birds. Which bird from this group in India can imitate the human voice?
(a) Hill Myna (*Gracula religiosa*) (b) Common Iora (*Aegithina tiphia*) (c) Shama (*Copsychus malabaricus*) (d) Carrion Crow (*Corvus corone*)

552. Which bird is considered the best songbird of India?
(a) Golden Oriole (*Oriolus oriolus*) (b) Redvented Bulbul (*Pycnonotus cafer*) (c) Spotted Babbler (*Pellorneum ruficeps*) (d) Shama (*Copsychus malabaricus*)

553. Of the 27 orders of the birds in the world, how many orders are found in India?
(a) 20   (b) 22   (c) 23   (d) 24

554. Of the 155 families of the birds in the world, how many are found in the Indian subcontinent?

(a) 50   (b) 60   (c) 77   (d) 102

555.   What is the excrement of sea birds called ?
       (a) Dung (b) Guano (c) Waste (d) No specific
       name

556.   To what use is Guano put ?
       (a) Manure (b) Medicine (c) Construction
       (d) Fuel

557.   Which birds' nests are used to prepare the
       Nest Soup?
       (a) Indian Ediblenest Swiftlet (*Collocalia
       unicolor*) (b) Alpine Swift (*Apus apus*)
       (c) Pallid Swift (*Apus pallidus*) (d) House Swift
       (*Apus affinis*)

558.   Out of ten species of Megapods (*Megapodidae*)
       in the world, how many are found in India?
       (a) 1 (b) 2 (c) 3 (d) 4

559.   Name the only group of birds whose legs are
       encased within the body down to the ankle
       joint:
       (a) Orioles (*Oriolidae*) (b) Divers (*Gavidae*)
       (c) Kingfishers (*Alcedinidae*) (d) Swifts
       (*Apodidae*)

560.   What is the habitat distribution of
       Narcondam Hornbill (*Rhyticeros plicatus
       narcondami*)?
       (a) Narcondam Islands (b) Kerala (c) M.P.
       (d) Himalayas

561.   Name the species of flightless bird other than
       the Siwalik Ostrich whose fossils have been
       found in the Siwalik hills:
       (a) Emu (*Dromaius sivalensis*) (b) Hoopoe
       (*Upupa epops*) (c) Fairy Bluebird (*Irena puella*)
       (d) No such fossil unearthed

562. Are *Pelecanus cautleyi* and *P. sivalensis* fossilized Pelicans found in the Siwalik hills?

(a) Yes (b) No

563. Name the bird which was found only in the Mussoorie and Naini Tal areas of Western Himalaya between 1650m and 2100m and currently the bird is considered as extinct:

(a) Wigeon (*Anas penelope*) (b) Pinkheaded Duck(*Rhodonessa caryophyllacea*) (c) Mountain Quail (*Ophrysia superciliosa*) (d) Whitewinged Wood Duck (*Cairina scutulata*)

564. Except the *Afropavo* of Africa, all species of Pheasants are confined to south-east Asia. How many species of Pheasants are found in the Himalayan region?

(a) 2 (b) 4 (c) 6 (d) 8

565. The range of distribution of which Junglefowl is remarkably associated with the teak (*Tectona grandis*) forests in India?

(a) Grey Junglefowl (*Gallus sonneratii*) (b) Red Junglefowl (*Gallus gallus*) (c) Chir Pheasant (*Catreus wallichii*) (d) Common Peafowl (*Pavo cristatus*)

566. The range of distribution of which Junglefowl is remarkably associated with the Sal (*Shorea robusta*) forests in India?

(a) Grey Junglefowl (*Gallus sonneratii*) (b) Red Junglefowl (*Gallus gallus*) (c) Chir Pheasant (*Catreus wallichii*) (d) Common Peafowl (*Pavo cristatus*)

567. What is the total number of bird forms found in the Indian subcontinent?

(a) 1700 (b) 2061 (c) 1961 (d) 2063

568. Incidental shooting of which bird inspired Salim Ali to become the world famous ornithologist?
(a) Crested Lark (*Galerida cristata*) (b) Redstart (*Phoenicurus ochruros*) (c) Yellowthroated Sparrow (*Petronia xanthocollis*) (d) Whitewinged Wood Duck (*Cairina scutulata*)

569. Of the 145 species of Waterfowls in the world, does any species has spotted eggs?
(a) Yes (b) No

570. Which bird was rediscovered a few years back in the Kumaon terai by the Bombay Natural History Society?
(a) Rock Sparrow (*Petronia petronia*) (b) Baya (*Ploceus philippinus*) (c) Finn's Baya (*P. megarhynchus*) (d) Scrub Sparrow (*Passer moabiticus*)

571. Which resident duck of tropical evergreen forests of North-east India is currently facing the threat of extinction?
(a) Spotbill Duck (*Anas poecilorhyncha*)
(b) Tree Duck (*Dendrocygna javanica*)
(c) Tufted Duck (*Aythya fuligula*)
(d) Whitewinged Wood Duck (*Cairina scutulata*)

572. Which Indian Duck currently under the threat of extinction is being bred in captivity at Slimbridge, U.K., to release subsequently in the wild?
(a) Pinkheaded Duck (*Rhodonessa caryophyllacea*) (b) Whitewinged Wood Duck

(*Cairina scutulata*) (c) Scaup Duck (*Aythya marila*) (d) Smew (*Mergus albellus*)

573. Which is the smallest Passerine bird in India?
(a) Tickell's Flowerpecker (*Dicaeum erythrorhynchos*) (b) Legge's Flowerpecker (*D. vincens*) (c) Red Munia (*Estrilda amandava*) (d) Green Munia (*E. formosa*)

574. Which is the largest Passerine (*perching*) bird in India?
(a) Raven (*Corvus corax*) (b) Jungle Crow (*Corvus macrorhynchos*) (c) Rook (*C. frugilegus*) (d) Carrian Crow (*C. corone*)

575. Which is the tallest Indian bird?
(a) Common Crane (*Grus grus*) (b) Hooded Crane (*Grus monacha*) (c) Demoiselle Crane (*Anthropoides virgo*) (d) Sarus Crane (*Grus antigone*)

576. Which Indian bird has the largest legs?
(a) Sarus Crane (*Grus antigone*)
(b) Blacknecked Crane (*Grus nigricollis*)
(c) Siberian Crane (*Grus leucogeranus*)
(d) Painted Stork (*Mycteria leucocephala*)

577. Identify the crane that breeds on India China borders, rendering it necessary to maintain close bilateral relations between the two countries to ensure the survival of the species:
(a) Blacknecked Crane (*Grus nigricollis*)
(b) Siberian Crane (*Grus leucogeranus*)
(c) Sarus Crane (*Grus antigone*) (d) Common Crane (*Grus grus*)

578. Name the world's tallest flying bird which occurs in India:
   (a) Blacknecked Crane (*Grus nigricollis*)
   (b) Siberian Crane (*Grus leucogeranus*)
   (c) Sarus Crane (*Grus antigone*) (d) Common Crane (*Grus grus*)

579. Identify the bird for which there are only two known wintering resorts left for the western race of this species; India is one of these places:
   (a) Siberian Crane (*Grus leucogeranus*)
   (b) Lesser Adjutant (*Leptoptilos javanicus*)
   (c) Spoonbill (*Platalea leucordia*) (d) Adjutant (*Leptoptilos dubius*)

580. Which bird in India is venerated and worshipped as a symbol of fidelity and family bondage?
   (a) Sarus (*Grus antigone*) (b) Common Peafowl (*Pavo cristatus*) (c) Indian Roller (*Coracias benghalensis*) (d) None of the above

581. Which Stork has the feeding habit of a Vulture?
   (a) Openbill Stork (*Anastomus oscitans*)
   (b) White Stork (*Ciconia ciconia*) (c) Black Stork (*C. nigra*) (d) Adjutant (*Leptoptilos dubius*)

582. What is the habitat distribution of the Hooded Crane (*Grus monacha*) in India?
   (a) North-eastern India (b) Deserts
   (c) Peninsular India (d) Central India

583. Is Sarus Crane (*Grus antigone*) endemic to India, i.e., found nowhere else in the world?
   (a) Yes (b) No

584. Of the total 14 species of Cranes in the world, how many are seen in the Indian subcontinent?
(a) 5 (b) 6 (c) 7 (d) 8

585. Is Common Crane (*Grus grus*) migratory to India?
(a) Yes (b) No

586. Is Demoiselle Crane (*Anthropoides virgo*) migratory to India?
(a) Yes (b) No

587. Is Siberian Crane (*Grus leucogeranus*) a resident bird of India?
(a) Yes (b) No

588. Is Hooded Crane (*Crus monacha*) a resident bird of India?
(a) Yes (b) No

589. Is Blacknecked Crane (*Grus nigricollis*) a resident bird of India?
(a) Yes (b) No

590. Where does the Blacknecked Crane (*Grus nigricollis*) breed?
(a) Ladakh (b) Bhutan (c) Kerala (d) Andaman & Nicobar Islands

591. How many breeding species of Storks are found in the Indian subcontinent?
(a) 6 (b) 8 (c) 12 (d) 14

592. Of the total 17 species of Storks in the world, Indian subcontinent has six resident Storks and is second to Africa only. How many species are found in Africa?
(a) 6 (b) 8 (c) 12 (d) 14

593. Out of four species of Flamingos (*Phoenicopteridae*) in the world how many are found in India?
   (a) 2 (b) 4 (c) 6 (d) 8

594. Where does the Flamingo (*Phoenicopterus roseus*) breed in India?
   (a) Great Runn of Kutch (b) M.P. (c) U.P. (d) Kerala

595. Is Lesser Flamingo (*Phoenicopterus minor*) found throughout India?
   (a) Yes (b) No

596. Where does the Lesser Flamingo breed?
   (a) Kutch (b) Himalayan Lakes (c) Ceylon (d) West Bengal

597. Which of the following birds has the bill curved down at an angle from about half its length?
   (a) Flamingo (*Phoenicopterus roseus*) (b) Rosy Pelican (*Pelecanus onocrotalus*) (c) Lesser Frigate Bird (*Fregata minor*) (d) Whooper Swan (*Cygnus cygnus*)

598. Is Flamingo (*Phoenicopterus roseus*) a very small bird?
   (a) Yes (b) No

599. Is Mute Swan (*Cygnus olor*) resident bird of India?
   (a) Yes (b) No

600. Is Dalmatian Pelican (*Pelecanus philippensis*) resident bird of India?
   (a) Yes (b) No

601. Of the world's seventeen species of Stork, how many are seen at Keoladeo Ghana National Park, Bharatpur?

(a) 5 (b) 6 (c) 7 (d) 8

602. How many species of Stork are migratory to India?

(a) 1 (b) 2 (c) 3 (d) 4

603. Which bird has long neck, long legs and heavy beak with black markings on white wings?

(a) Painted Stork (*Mycteria leucocephala*)

(b) Openbilled Stork (*Anastomus oscitans*)

(c) Whitenecked Stork (*Ciconia episcopus*)

(d) Blacknecked Stork (*Ephippiorhynchus asiaticus*)

604. Which tree provides the nesting habitat for most of the breeding bird populations of Stork at Keoladeo Ghana National Park, Bharatpur?

(a) Babul (*Acacia nilotica*) (b) Pongum (*Pongamea pinnata*) (c) Neem (*Melia azadirachta*) (d) Khair (*Acacia catechu*)

605. To which season of the year the breeding season of birds at Keoladeo Ghana National Park chiefly coincides?

(a) Winter (b) Monsoon (c) Summer (d) No well defined season

606. Which group of birds display the behaviour of bowing and beak-clattering while changing the duties at nest?

(a) Stork (b) Crane (c) Duck (d) Flamingo

607. Which Stork has arched mandibles, thus creating a gap between upper and lower mandibles?

(a) Openbill Stork (*Anastomus oscitans*)

(b) Whitenecked Stork (*Ciconia episcopus*)

(c) Sarus Crane (*Grus antigone*) (d) No such bird exists

608. What is a curious habit of the Openbill Stork (*Anastomus oscitans*)?
(a) Regurgitation of water over the eggs (b) Up-Down Display (c) Both (a) and (b) (d) None of the above

609. Is Painted Stork (*Mycteria lecocephala*) a colonial breeder?
(a) Yes (b) No

610. Is Openbill Stork a colonial nester?
(a) Yes (b) No

611. Are Whitenecked Stork (*Ciconia episcopus*) and the Blacknecked Stork (*Ephippiorhynchus asiaticus*) solitary birds?
(a) Yes (b) No

612. Does Blacknecked Stork display the 'greeting ceremony' by beak clattering and touching of wings?
(a) Yes (b) No

613. How many species of cormorants (*Phalacro coracidae*) breed at Keoladeo Ghana National Park, Bharatpur?
(a) 1 (b) 2 (c) 3 (d) 4

614. Which bird is called the Snake-bird?
(a) Darter (*Anhinga rufa*) (b) Little Cormorant (*Phalacrocorax niger*) (c) Indian Shag (*P. fuscicollis*) (d) Common Cormorant (*P. carbo*)

615. Which group of birds are called *Pan-kauwa* or the water-crow?
(a) Cormorants (b) Ducks (c) Kingfishers (d) Darters

616. Which bird has the typical feeding habit by harpooning fish?
(a) Darter (*Anhinga rufa*) (b) Little Cormorant (*Phalacrocorax niger*) (c) Indian Shag (*P. fuscicollis*) (d) Common Cormorant (*P. carbo*)

617. Is it true that Spoonbill (*Platalea leucordia*) and Ibis (*Threskiornis sp.*) have bred and produced hybrids in captivity?
(a) Yes (b) No

618. Which Indian bird has a spatulate bill?
(a) Spoon bill (*Platalea leucordia*) (b) White Ibis (*Threskiornis aethiopia*) (c) Black Ibis (*Pseudibis palillosa*) (d) Glossy Ibis (*Plegadis falcinellus*)

619. Do Ibises (*Threskiornithidae*) have down curved long bills?
(a) Yes (b) No

620. Range and numbers of many aquatic birds (*water birds*) have reduced due to which of the following factor/factors?
(a) Wetland drainage (b) Shooting (c) Pesticides (d) All the above

621. Which Egret in India develops the golden plumage on the head and neck during the breeding season?
(a) Intermediate Egret (*Egretta intermedia*) (b) Cattle Egret (*Bubulcus ibis*) (c) Large Egret (*Egretta alba*) (d) Paddy Bird (*Ardeola grayii*)

622. Of the total 14 species of Crane in the world, 6 are to be found in India. How many are to be seen at Keoladeo Ghana National Park, Bharatpur?
(a) 4   (b) 5   (c) 6   (d) 7

623. Reasons for large congregations of Sarus Crane (*Grus antigone*) during March-April are yet to be explained. Who describes this phenomenon as a 'gathering of the clans'?
(a) Salim Ali (b) Z. Futehally (c) Sir Martin Ewans (d) Bittu Sahgal

624. Where does the Sarus Crane build nest?
(a) Tree tops (b) Shallow water (c) Deserts (d) Cavities

625. How many eggs are normally laid by the Sarus Crane (*Grus antigone*)?
(a) 1 (b) 2 (c) 3 (d) 4

626. Is it true that chicks of the Sarus Crane (*Grus antigone*) freeze themselves when alarmed by parents for an approaching danger?
(a) Yes (b) No

627. Who wrote 'this crane is a cynosure of Bharatpur' about the Siberian White Crane (*Grus leucogeranus*)?
(a) Salim Ali (b) Sir Martin Ewans (c) Kailash Sankhala (d) J.C. Daniel

628. What is the chief food of the Siberian Crane (*Grus leucogeranus*)?
(a) Vegetation (b) Insect (c) Fish (d) Frog

629. Where are the breeding grounds of the Siberian Crane (*Grus leucogeranus*) located?
(a) NE Yakutia between Rivers Yana and Kelyne (b) Lower reaches of River Ob (c) Bharatpur (d) (a) and (b) both

630. Where are the headquarters of the International Crane Foundation located?
(a) Wisconsin (b) New Delhi (c) Washington (d) Gland

631. In which year, for the first time, International Crane Foundation, Wisconsin, bred successfully one Siberian Crane (*Grus leucogeranus*) in captivity through artificial insemination and incubation?
(a) 1960 (b) 1971 (c) 1081 (d) 1990

632. Which species of bird is being used as the foster mother for incubating the eggs of the Siberian Crane (*Grus leucogeranus*) to reduce mortality?
(a) Demoiselle Crane (*Anthropoides virgo*)
(b) Sarus Crane (*Grus antigone*) (c) Hooded Crane (*Grus monacha*) (d) Common Crane (*Grus grus*)

633. Where are the breeding colonies of the White or Rosy Pelican (*Pelecanus onocrotalus*) located in India?
(a) Runn of Kutch (b) Nelapattu (c) Point Calimere (d) No colony in India

634. What is the breeding colony of the Flamingos called?
(a) Flamingo Village (b) Flamingo City (c) Flamingo Camp (d) Flamingo Roost

635. What is the chief nest building material of Flamingos?
(a) Mud (b) Dry Twigs (c) Grass (d) Feathers and Dry Twigs

636. In which bird do you find a sieve-like bill especially adapted for aquatic habits?
(a) Flamingo (b) Duck (c) Goose (d) Cormorant

637. What is the Indian name given to the Flamingos?

(a) *Hans* (b) *Rajhans* (c) *Tota* (d) *Battakh*

638. In which schedule of the Wildlife (Protection) Act, 1972, are the Blacknecked, Hooded and Siberian Crane listed?
(a) 1 (b) 2 (c) 3 (d) 4

639. In which schedule of the Wildlife (Protection) Act, 1972, is the Eastern White Stork (*Ciconia ciconia boyciana*) listed?
(a) 1 (b) 2 (c) 3 (d) 4

640. In which schedule of the Wildlife (Protection) Act, 1972, is the White Spoonbill listed?
(a) 1 (b) 2 (c) 3 (d) 4

641. In which schedule of the Wildlife (Protection) Act, 1972, is the Nicobar Megapode (*Megapodius freycinet*) listed?
(a) 1 (b) 2 (c) 3 (d) 4

642. Name the Bustard found in the terai grasslands all along the southern edge of Himalayan foothills in isolated areas:
(a) Bengal Florican (*Eupodotis bengalensis*)
(b) Great Indian Bustard (*Choriotis nigriceps*)
(c) Lesser Florican (*Sypheotides indica*)
(d) Houbara (*Chlamydotis undulata*)

643. There are 22 species of Bustards (*Otididae*) in the world. How many species are found in India?
(a) 4   (b) 5   (c) 6   (d) 7

644. Which is the largest Bustard in India?
(a) Great Indian Bustard (*Choriotis nigriceps*)
(b) Houbara (*Chlamydotis undulata*) (c) Bengal Florican (*Eupodotis bengalensis*) (d) Lesser Florican (*Sypheotides indica*)

645. Which Bustard in India is known as Likh?
(a) Great Indian Bustard (*Choriotis nigriceps*)
(b) Houbara (*Chlamydotis undulata*) (c) Bengal
Florican (*Eupodotis bengalensis*) (d) Lesser
Florican (*Sypheotides indica*)

646. Where does the Houbara (*Chlamydotis undulata*) breed?
(a) India (b) Baluchistan (c) Africa (d) Ceylon

647. In which schedule of the Wildlife (Protection) Act, 1972, are Bustards listed?
(a) 1 (b) 2 (c) 3 (d) 4

648. Where does a Hornbill choose its nest site?
(a) Tree Cavity (b) Tree top (c) Dry Ground
(d) Shallow Water

649. After the mating, the female locks herself in the nest cavity in a tree trunk using her droppings to plaster the entrance. She stays inside the nest till young ones are 15 days old, and then breaks down the wall and comes out. Which bird has this peculiar nesting habit?
(a) Tit (b) Barbet (c) Hornbill
(d) Woodpecker

650. Which is the largest Hornbill in India?
(a) Great Pied Hornbill (*Buceros bicornis*)
(b) Rufousnecked Hornbill (*Aceros nipalensis*)
(c) Wreathed Hornbill (*Rhyticeros undulatus*)
(d) Malabar Pied Hornbill (*Anthracoceros coronatus*)

651. Is Narcondam Hornbill (*Rhyticeros plicatus*) endemic to Narcondam Island, India?
(a) Yes (b) No

652. Why are the Hornbills so named?

(a) Presence of hornlike bill (b) Presence of casque on the upper mandible (c) (a) & (b) both (d) None of the above

653. Which Indian bird has the widest wing span?
(a) Lammergeier (*Gypaetus barbatus*) (b) Himalayan Griffon (*Gyps himalayensis*) (c) King Vulture (*Sarcogyps calvus*) (d) Indian Whitebacked Vulture (*Gyps bengalensis*)

654. Name the bird which feeds only on bone-marrow and looks like an eagle but actually does not belong to that group?
(a) Lammergeier (*Gypaetus barbatus*) (b) Himalayan Griffon (*Gyps himalayensis*) (c) King Vulture (*Sarcogyps calvus*) (d) Indian Whitebacked Vulture (*Gyps bengalensis*)

655. Is Lammergeier also known as the Bearded Vulture?
(a) Yes (b) No

656. This bird collected during Travancore Bird Survey was misidentified by two great ornithologists of the world. Dr. Salim Ali misidentified it as Crested Hawk Eagle and H. Whistler as Jerdon's Baza. It was later identified at British Museum of Natural History. It is one of the rarest birds of prey in the world. Identify it:
(a) Feathertoed Hawk Eagle (*Spizaetus nipalensis kelaarti*) (b) Shorttoed Eagle (*Circaetus gallicus*) (c) Golden Eagle (*Aquila chrysaetos*) (d) Imperial Eagle (*Aquila heliaca*)

657. For a species of Vulture which also occurs in India, reintroduction is being resorted to

ensure the survival in Europe. The site selected by the World Wide Fund for Nature is Alps mountains. Name this species:

(a) Scavenger Vulture (*Neophron percnopterus*)
(b) Cinereous Vulture (*Aegypius monachus*)
(c) King Vulture (*Sarcogyps calvus*)
(d) Bearded Vulture (*Gypaetus barbatus*)

658. What is the speed of the world's fastest moving animal, the Peregrine Falcon (*Falco peregrinus*)?

(a) 350 km/h (b) 400 km/h (c) 100 km/h
(d) 50 km/h

659. Name the only Falcon known to build its nest:

(a) Hobby (*Falco subbuteo*) (b) Redheaded Merlin (*Falco chicquera*) (c) Redlegged Falcon (*Falco vespertinus*) (d) Kestrel (*Falco tinnunculus*)

660. The Himalayas present a hurdle for migratory birds from Central Asia, and many casualties occur. Name the bird found frozen dead near the Everest at an altitude of 8000m:

(a) Imperial Eagle (*Aquila heliaca*) (b) Steppe Eagle (*Aquila rapax*) (c) Greater Spotted Eagle (*Aquila clanga*)

661. Pinkheaded Duck (*Rhodonessa caryophyllacea*) is supposedly extinct. When was it last sighted?

(a) 1930 (b) 1935 (c) 1940 (d) 1945

662. Which species of duck may be misidentified by casual bird-watchers as the Pinkheaded Duck (*Rhodonessa caryophyllacea*)?

(a) Red Crested Pochard (*Netta rufina*) (b) Gadwall (*Anas strepera*) (c) Wigeon (*Anas penelope*) (d) Mallard (*Anas platyrhynchos*)

663. What was the peak geological time of bird diversity?
(a) Pleistocene (b) Miocene (c) Eocene (d) Paleocene

664. Is it true that Megapodes do not incubate eggs by means of parental body heat and when eggs hatch, the young ones are able to run within a few hours and fly within a day?
(a) Yes (b) No

665. Within the Indian limits where does the Ruddy Shelduck (*Tadorna ferrugenea*) breed?
(a) Ladakh (b) M.P. (c) Rajasthan (d) Tamil Nadu

666. Which of the following ducks is exclusive to the Indian subcontinent?
(a) Spotbill Duck (*Anas poecilorhyncha poecilorhyncha*) (b) Ruddy Shelduck (*Tadorna ferrugenea*) (c) Pintail (*Anas acuta*) (d) Cotton Teal (*Nettapus coromandelianus*)

667. From which part of the world does migratory population of Pintail come to India?
(a) Caspian Region and Siberia (b) China (c) Pakistan (d) Brazil

668. Male individual of which species of Duck has a knob on its bill?
(a) Large Whistling Teal (*Dendrocygna bicolor*)
(b) Comb Duck (*Sarkidiornis melanotus*)
(c) Baikal Teal (*Anas formosa*) (d) Tree Duck (*Dendrocygna javanica*)

669. How many species of Jacana are found in India?
(a) 1 (b) 2 (c) 3 (d) 4

670. Where is the nest of a Jacana placed?
(a) Floating aquatic vegetation (b) Tree cavities (c) Tree tops (d) Ground scrap

671. Is Marsh Harrier (*Circus aeruginosus*) a winter migrant to India from Europe and Mongolia?
(a) Yes (b) No

672. Name a resident Eagle of India having prominent fan-shaped crest of black feathers with white bars along the edge?
(a) Crested Serpent Eagle (*Spilornis cheela*) (b) Crested Hawk-Eagle (*Spizaetus chirrhatus*) (c) Tawny Eagle (*Aquila rapax*) (d) Black Eagle (*Ictinaetus malayensis*)

673. Where does the long-legged Buzzard (*Buteo rufinus*) breed?
(a) Himalayas (b) Satpuras (c) Vindhyas (d) Western Ghats

674. What is the food habit of the Vultures?
(a) Grain-feeder (b) Carrion-feeder (c) Insect eater (d) Fish-eater

675. Which organisation recently rediscovered the Jerdon s or Double-banded Courser after 86 years of its last sighting?
(a) Bombay Natural History Society (b) World Wide Fund for Nature (c) Wildlife Preservation Society of India (d) Birdwatchers Society of India

676. Which Stork has adapted to scavenger feeding habit?

(a) Adjutant Stork (*Leptoptilos dubius*)
(b) Openbilled Stork (*Anastomus osciatus*)
(c) Painted Stork (*Mycteria leucocephala*)
(d) None of the above

677. What is the diagnostic feature of the Adjutant Stork?
(a) Large, yellow wedge-shaped bill
(b) Long pendent pouch   (c) (a) & (b) both

678. When was the Mountain Quail (*Ophrysia superciliosa*) last sighted?
(a) 1876 (b) 1890 (c) 1900 (d) 1950

679. What kind of nests are prepared by Quails and Junglefowls?
(a) Scraps on the ground, lined with grass (b) Twig nests in tree tops (c) Cavity nests in tree trunks   (d) Tunnel nests in earth banks

680. What kind of nests are prepared by Crows, Kites, Doves, Vultures, Cormorants and Storks?
(a) Scraps on the ground, lined with grass
(b) Twig nests in tree tops (c) Cavity nests in tree trunks (d) Tunnel nests in earth banks

681. What is the nest site selected by the Woodpeckers, Barbets, Hornbills, Owls, Mynas and Ducks?
(a) Cavities in the tree trunk (b) Tree tops
(c) Mud nest on the ground (d) None of the above

682. Which of the following group of birds are primary cavity nesters, i.e., they excavate the cavities?
(a) Woodpeckers (b) Parakeets (c) Barbets
(d) All of them

683. Which of the following **group of birds** are secondary cavity nesters, i.e., they re-use the cavities excavated by primary cavity nester?
(a) Mynas (b) Owls (c) Hornbills (d) All of them

684. What kind of nest is prepared by Bee-eaters, Kingfishers and Hoopoe?
(a) Mud nest (b) Tree cavity nest (c) Tunnel nest in earth banks (d) Cupshaped nest of grass

685. Nests built entirely of mud are prepared by which group of birds?
(a) Weaver birds (b) Tailor birds (c) Wren Warblers (d) Whistling Thrush, Black Birds, Swallows and Martins

686. What kind of nests do Weaverbirds, Sunbirds and Flowerpeckers make?
(a) Pendent nest (b) Domed nest (c) Cupshaped nest (d) Twig platform nest

687. What is the nest of the Tailor Bird?
(a) Pendent Nest (b) Domed Nest (c) Nest in leaves stitched together (d) Mud Nest

688. Which group of birds show nest parasitism?
(a) Hornbills (b) Barbets (c) Cuckoos (d) Cranes

689. Koel (*Eudynamys scolopacea*) does not build its nest. Nest of which bird is utilized by Koel for egg-laying?
(a) House Crow (*Corvus splendens*) (b) Jungle Crow (*C. macrorhynchos*) (c) (a) & (b) both (d) Koel does not require a nest

690. What is the term given to flight involving sailing on outstretched motionless wings?

(a) Gliding (b) Soaring (c) Flapping (d) Hovering

691. How does *soaring* differs from *gliding* in birds?
(a) *Thermals* help in soaring (b) *Thermals* help in gliding and not in soaring (c) No difference

692. Which Indian bird sometimes use the hovering flight?
(a) Kestrel (*Falco tinnunculus*) (b) Pied King-fisher (*Ceryle rudis*) (c) Black-winged Kite (*Elanus caeruleus*) (d) All above

693. Which species of Owlet now considered as extinct was last sighted in the year 1914?
(a) Forest Spotted Owlet (*Athena blewitti*) (b) Spotted Owlet (*Athene brama*) (c) Barred Owlet (*Glaucidium cuculoides*) (d) Jungle Owlet (*G. radiatum*)

694. Which Indian bird is believed to migrate from its Himalayan breeding grounds to the Nilgiris involving a non-stop flight of about 2400 km?
(a) Woodcock (*Scolopax rusticola*) (b) Gadwall (*Anas strepera*) (c) Common Teal (*Anas crecca*) (d) Honey Buzzard (*Pernis ptilorhyncus*)

695. Is it true that the Great Indian Bustard (*Choriotis nigriceps*) was once common on the grassy plains of India, but because of the land diversion for agriculture and direct poaching brought the numbers nearing extinction. However, now strict habitat protection measures have saved it from going into oblivion?

(a) Yes (b) No

696. What was the basic reason for extinction of the Pinkheaded Duck (*Rhodonessa caryophyllacea*)?
(a) Uncontrolled shooting (b) Racial senescence (c) Habitat destruction (d) No apparent cause

697. What is the State bird of Madhya Pradesh?
(a) Verditer Flycature (*Muscicapa thalassina*)
(b) Paradise Flycature (*Terpsiphone paradisi*)
(c) Blacknaped Blue Flycature (*Monarcha azurea*) (d) Crested Bunting (*Melophus lathami*)

698. What is the State bird of Uttar Pradesh?
(a) Sarus Crane (*Grus antigone*) (b) Great Indian Bustard (*Choriotis nigriceps*) (c) Spotted Munia (*Lonchura punctulata*) (d) Brahminy Duck (*Tadorna ferrugenea*)

699. What is the State bird of Rajasthan?
(a) Sarus Crane (*Grus antigone*) (b) Great Indian Bustard (*Choriotis nigriceps*) (c) Spotted Munia (*Lonchura punctulata*) (d) Brahminy Duck (*Tadorna ferrugenea*)

700. What is the State bird of Himachal Pradesh?
(a) Monal Pheasant (*Lophophorus impejanus*)
(b) Chir Pheasant (*Catreus wallichii*) (c) Kalij Pheasant (*Lophura leucomelana*) (d) None of the above

701. Is it true that Indian bird fauna has strong affinity with African and Indo-Chinese bird fauna and very few species are related to the palaearctic regions?
(a) Yes (b) No

702. Which introduced species (exotic) of Sparrow has started breeding in India?
(a) Java Sparrow (*Padda oryzivora*) (b) House Sparrow (*Passer domesticus*) (c) Scrub Sparrow (*Passer moabiticus*) (d) None of the above

703. How many species of birds of prey are found in India?
(a) 60 (b) 70 (c) 80 (d) 90

704. *Falconidae* and *Accipitridae* are birds of prey in India. What is the distribution of species in these families?
(a) *Falconidae*—12 and *Accipitridae*—48
(b) *Falconidae*—48 and *Accipitridae*—12
(c) *Falconidae*—10 and *Accipitridae*—40
(d) *Falconidae*—15 and *Accipitridae*—20

705. In which schedule of the Wildlife (Protection) Act, 1972, are various Pheasants listed?
(a) 1 (b) 2 (c) 3 (d) 4

706. Name the only vulture listed in Schedule 1 of the Wildlife (Protection) Act, 1972:
(a) Whitebacked Vulture (*Gyps bengalensis*)
(b) King Vulture (*Sarcogyps calvus*)
(c) Bearded Vulture or Lammergeier (*Gypaetus barbatus*) (d) None

707. How many species of *Tragopan* are listed in Schedule 1 of the Wildlife (Protection) Act, 1972?
(a) 2 (b) 3 (c) 4 (d) 5

708. What is the range of distribution of the only Lorikeet of India—Indian Lorikeet (*Loriculus vernalis*)?

(a) Eastern Himalaya (b) North-eastern Himalaya (c) Eastern Ghats, Western Ghats & Andaman & Nicobar Islands (d) (a), (b) & (c) all

709. Which is the largest Parakeet in India?
(a) Nicobar Parakeet (*Psittacula caniceps*)
(b) Alexandrine Parakeet (*P. eupatria*)
(c) Slatyheaded Parakeet (*P. himalayana*)
(d) Redbreasted Parakeet (*P. alexandri*)

710. Which is the largest Woodpecker in India?
(a) Himalayan Great Slaty Woodpecker (*Mulleripicus pulverulentus*) (b) Indian Great Black Woodpecker (*Dryocopus javensis*) (c) Scalybilled Green Woodpecker (*Picus squamatus*) (d) Large Yellownaped Woodpecker (*Picus flavinucha*)

8

THE REPTILES

711. What do you understand by the term reptile?
(a) Creeping animal (b) Cold-blooded animal (c) Running animal (d) Arboreal animal

712. There are about 6000 species of reptiles in the world. How many are found in India?
(a) 300 (b) 440 (c) 540 (d) 640

713. Which is the largest Crocodile in the world?
(a) Estuarine Crocodile (*Crocodylus porosus*)
(b) Gharial (*Gavialis gangeticus*) (c) Marsh Crocodile (*Crocodylus palustris*) (d) None of the above

714. Name the only state of India where all the three species of Crocodiles are found:
(a) M.P. (b) U.P. (c) Orissa (d) Rajasthan

715. What is the food habit of Crocodiles?
(a) Herbivorous (b) Carnivorous (c) Omnivorous (d) Caprophagous

716. What is the colour of Crocodile eggs?
(a) White (b) Blue (c) Grey (d) Violet

717. Do Alligators occur in India?
(a) Yes (b) No

718. Is it true that Crocodile teeth are shed and replaced periodically throughout the life?
(a) Yes (b) No

719. Which is the most widely distributed Crocodile in India?
(a) Marsh Crocodile (*Crocodylus palustris*)
(b) Estuarine Crocodile (*Crocodylus porosus*)
(c) Long-snouted Crocodile (*Gavialis gangeticus*)

720. How many species of Crocodiles are found in India?
(a) 1 (b) 2 (c) 3 (d) 4

721. Do Muggar (*Crocodylus palustris*) and Estuarine Crocodile (*Crocodylus porosus*) have overlapping range of distribution?
(a) Yes (b) No

722. Is it true that Muggar or Marsh Crocodile (*Crocodylus palustris*) was once distributed throughout the Indian subcontinent but due to multi-site local extinction the population has drastically dwindled?
(a) Yes (b) No

723. Which part of the body of Muggar (*Crocodylus palustris*) acts as propellent during swimming?

(a) Tail (b) Fore legs (c) Hind legs (d) Not known

724. Where does the mating of Muggar (*Crocodylus palustris*) take place?
(a) Water (b) Land (c) Tree (d) Not known

725. Where does the female Muggar lay eggs?
(a) Pit nest prepared on the bank (b) Inside the water (c) On tree tops (d) On bare rocks

726. What is the number of eggs laid in a clutch by Muggar (*Crocodylus palustris*)?
(a) 3 to 50 (b) 20 to 60 (c) 60 to 100 (d) More than 1000

727. What is the incubation period of the Muggar (*Crocodylus palustris*)?
(a) 2 to 3 months (b) 3 to 4 months (c) 10 days (d) 20 days

728. What is the cause of the depletion and endangering of the Muggar (*Crocodylus palustris*) in India?
(a) Commercial hunting for skin (b) Habitat destruction (c) Egg collection (d) All above

729. What is the distribution of the salt water Crocodile (*Crocodylus porosus*)?
(a) Tidal estuaries of continental rivers (b) Freshwater inland lakes (c) Freshwater rivers (d) Forests of central India

730. What is the cause of local extinction of salt water Crocodile (*Crocodylus porosus*)?
(a) Hunting for skin (b) Loss of breeding habitat (c) Egg collection (d) (a) & (b) both

731. What is the difference between the nesting habit of the Muggar (*Crocodylus palustris*) and Estuarine Crocodile (*Crocodylus porosus*)?

(a) Estuarine Crocodile builds a mound nest (b) Nest of Estuarine Crocodile is made of vegetation and mud heaped on the ground (c) Muggar digs a pit nest in the sandy banks of streams and tanks (d) All above show the difference

732. What is the average clutch size of eggs in the Estuarine Crocodile (*Crocodylus porosus*)?
(a) 50 eggs (b) 100 eggs (c) 200 eggs (d) 400 eggs

733. What is the incubation period for the eggs of Estuarine Crocodile (*Crocodylus porosus*)?
(a) 30 to 40 days (b) 30 to 60 days (c) 60 to 70 days (d) 80 to 90 days

734. After eggs hatch, how the Crocodile hatchlings reach water?
(a) Hatchlings crawl to water (b) Female carries hatchlings in the mouth to water (c) Female carries hatchlings on her back to water (d) No specific behaviour seen

735. How long does Estuarine Crocodile (*Crocodylus porosus*) mother provides parental care to its hatchlings?
(a) 70 days (b) 100 days (c) 150 days (d) 200 days

736. How Gharial or Longsnouted Crocodile (*Gavialis gangeticus*) can be distinguished from Muggar and Estuarine Crocodile?
(a) Gharial has long snout (b) Gharial is longer than the other two (c) Gharial is fish-eater (d) None of the above

737. What is the distribution of Gharial (*Gavialis gangeticus*) in India?
(a) Ganges, Brahmaputra and the Mahanadi river systems (b) Kaveri, Krishna and the

Godavari river systems (c) Inland lakes of central India (d) Tidal estuaries of peninsular rivers

738. What kind of nest does Gharial (*Gavialis gangeticus*) make?
(a) Pit nest in sandy banks (b) Mound nest in banks (c) Nest inside the water (d) Not known

739. In what form does Gharial (*Gavialis gangeticus*) provide parental care to its youngs?
(a) Nest protection (b) Release of youngs into water (c) Guarding of hatchlings (d) All above

740. Which are the egg predators of Crocodiles in India?
(a) Monitor Lizard (b) Pigs and rats (c) Jackals (d) All above

741. Owing to the hunting for skin and loss of habitat due to damming of rivers, population of Gharial (*Gavialis gangeticus*) was dwindling. What was the management strategy followed to help conserve the species?
(a) Wild egg collection, captive rearing and release into the wild (b) Strict protection against hunting (c) Habitat conservation (d) All above conservation efforts

742. Which is the largest of all living chelonians (*turtles and tortoise*) next only to the Estuarine Crocodile (*Crocodylus porosus*) ?
(a) Loggerhead Turtle (*Caretta caretta*)
(b) Leatherback Sea Turtle (*Demochelys coriacea*)
(c) Green Turtle (*Chelonia mydas*) (d) Olive Ridley Turtle (*Lepidochelys olivacea*)

743. How many species of marine Turtles are recorded from Indian waters?

(a) 5 (b) 6 (c) 7 (d) 8

744. Which is the rarest marine Turtle in Indian waters?
(a) Loggerhead (*Caretta caretta*) (b) Green Turtle (*Chelonia mydas*) (c) Olive Ridley Turtle (*Lepidochelys olivacea*) (d) Leatherback Turtle (*Dermochelys coriacea*)

745. Which is the smallest marine Turtle?
(a) Loggerhead (*Caretta caretta*) (b) Green Turtle (*Chelonia mydas*) (c) Olive Ridley Turtle (*Lepidochelys olivacea*) (d) Leatherback Turtle (*Dermochelys coriacea*)

746. Are the Pacific Turtle and Olive Loggerhead synonymous to the Olive Ridley Turtle (*Lepidochelys olivacea*)?
(a) Yes (b) No

747. What is the main food of the Green Turtle (*Chelonia mydas*)?
(a) Marine algae (b) Marine crustaceans (c) Fish (d) Insects

748. What is the nesting habitat of the sea Turtles?
(a) Beaches with light sand (b) Deep sea (c) Island forests (d) Not recorded

749. What kind of nest is prepared by the Green Turtle (*Chelonia mydas*)?
(a) Sand pit nest (b) Vegetation mound nest (c) Twig platform (d) Rubble mound nest

750. What is the average clutch size of the Green Turtle (*Chelonia mydas*)?
(a) 105 eggs (b) 110 eggs (c) 120 eggs (d) 200 eggs

751. What is the incubation period in Green Turtle (*Chelonia mydas*)?

(a) 45 days in warmer months and 70 days in colder months (b) 70 days in warmer months and 100 days in colder month (c) 30 days (d) 200 days

752. What is the food habit of the Olive Ridley Turtle (*Lepidochelys olivacea*)?
(a) Herbivorous (b) Carnivorous (c) Omnivorous (d) Insectivorous

753. Which is the most common shore nesting marine Turtle in India?
(a) Olive Ridley Turtle (*Lepidochelys olivacea*)
(b) Hawksbill Turtle (*Eretmochelys imbricata*)
(c) Green Turtle (*Chelonia mydas*) (d) None of the above

754. What is the curious nesting behaviour of Olive Ridley Turtle (*Lepidochelys olivacea*)?
(a) Nest covering with vegetation (b) Open nests (c) Incubation by parental heat (d) Nest guarding

755. Is it true that Green Turtle (*Chelonia mydas*) is the most valuable of all living reptiles because of its exploitation for meat, soup, eggs and oil?
(a) Yes (b) No

756. Is Green Sea Turtle (*Chelonia mydas*) also known as Sunray Turtle?
(a) Yes (b) No

757. Where is the world's largest known nesting site of Olive Ridley Turtle (*Lepidochelys olivacea*) located?
(a) Andaman & Nicobar Islands (b) Kerala beaches (c) Gahiramata beach, Orissa (d) Northern coast of Sri Lanka

758. 'Carey' is derived from the flexible horny coverings of the carapace of which sea Turtle?
(a) Olive Ridley Turtle (*Lepidochelys olivacea*)
(b) Hawksbill Turtle (*Eretmochelys imbricata*)
(c) Loggerhead (*Caretta caretta*) (d) All sea Turtles

759. For what purpose is 'carey' used?
(a) Jewellery making (b) Medicine (c) Cosmetics
(d) Food

760. Is Hawksbill Turtle (*Eretmochelys imbricata*) also known as Caret and Tortoise Shell Turtle?
(a) Yes (b) No

761. Where are the nesting sites of Hawksbill Turtle (*Eretmochelys imbricata*) located?
(a) Andaman & Nicobar Islands (b) Tamil Nadu
(c) Karnataka (d) West Bengal

762. What is the average clutch size of the Hawksbill Turtle (*Eretmochelys imbricata*)?
(a) 10 eggs (b) 20 eggs (c) 40 eggs (d) 100 eggs

763. What is the food habit of the Hawksbill Turtle?
(a) Herbivorous (b) Carnivorous (c) Omnivorous
(d) Not known

764. Of the 5 recorded species of marine Turtles in India, how many nest on the Indian beaches?
(a) 5 (b) 4 (c) 3 (d) 1

765. What is the difference between land Tortoise and Terrapins?
(a) Terrapins are aquatic creatures (b) Terrapins have flattened limbs and webbed digits (c) (a) & (b) both (d) No difference

766. Which is the most widely distributed Terrapin in India?
(a) Indian Pond Terrapin (*Melanochelys trijuga*)
(b) Roofed Terrapin (*Kachuga tecta*) (c) Smith's

Terrapin (*K. smithi*) (d) Dhoor Terrapin
(*K. dhongoka*)

767. Which freshwater Terrapin is known from two
specimens collected from the dense forests of
Kerala? It was rediscovered in the year 1982
from Chalakudy forests in Kerala:
(a) Forest Cane Turtle (*Heosemys silvatica*)
(b) Kerala Forest Terrapin (c) (a) and (b) are
synonymous (d) Batagur Terrapin (*Batagur
baska*)

768. What is the identification feature of the Starred
Tortoise (*Geochelone elegans*)?
(a) Radiating yellow streaks on the domed
carapace (b) Large size of shell (c) Red colour
which changes according to sunlight (d) Star-
shaped body

769. Which of the following Tortoise is a fossil
recovered from the Siwalik Hills?
(a) *Colossochelys atlas* (b) *Geochelone atlas* (c) (a) &
(b) are synonymous (d) *Geochelone elegans*

770. The Golden Hill Gecko (*Calodactylodes aureus*) is
the only representative of the genus and is a
rare lizard. Where is it found?
(a) Tirumalai Hills, Andhra Pradesh (b) Satpura
Hills, M.P. (c) Annamalai Hills,Tamil Nadu
(d) Vindhya Hills, M.P.-Rajasthan

771. Gliding Gecko (*Ptychozoon kuhli*), a 190-cm-long
creature, has webbed toes and skin flaps on the
sides of the entire body including tail. Where is
it found?
(a) Nicobar Islands (b) North-eastern India
(c) Thar Desert (d) Deccan Peninsula

772. Though most lizards are harmless but one species of *Gekko* found in Assam and nearby area can bark and bite like a dog. It feeds on rats, insects and even snakes. Name the species:

(a) Tokay or Tuctoo (*Gekko gecko*) (b) Andaman Emerald Gecko (*Phelsuma andamanensis*) (c) Banded Rock Gecko (*Cyrtodactylus dekkanensis*) (d) Bark Gecko (*Hemidactylus leschenaulti*)

773. Which Lizard is believed to reproduce without mating and fertilization?

(a) *Hemidactylus garnoti* (b) *Gekko gecko* (c) *Hemidactylus brooki* (d) No such creature exists

774. Name the only Lizard in India with eyelids:

(a) Fat-tailed Gecko (*Eublepharis macularis*) (b) Gliding Gecko (*Ptychozoon kuhli*) (c) Termite Hill Gecko (*Hemidactylus triedrus*) (d) Garden Gecko (*Calodactylodes aureus*)

775. Is Common Garden Lizard (*Calotes versicolor*) and Bloodsucker synonyms?

(a) Yes (b) No

776. Name an arboreal tree Skink, hitherto believed to be endemic to Sri Lanka, which was photographed in Mundanthurai by Dr. A. J. T. Johnsingh of the Wildlife Institute of India, Dehra Dun.

(a) *Dasia haliana* (b) Snake Skink (*Riopa punctata*) (c) Common Skink (*Mabuya carinata*) (d) Sandfish (*Ophiomorus tridactylus*)

777. Name the desert Lizard whose tail is considered a delicacy. As a result of over-exploitation it has become rare and has been included in Schedule 1 of the Wildlife (Protection) Act, 1972:

(a) Spiny-tailed Lizard (*Uromastyx hardwickii*)
(b) Fanthroated Lizard (*Sitana ponticeriana*) (c)
Flying Lizard (*Draco dussumieri*) (d) Blue-throated
Lizard (*Ptyctolaemus gularis*)

778. Flying Dragons (*Draco sp.*) provide the unique
example of discontinuous distribution to the
zoogeographers. In India one species is found in
south Indian hills (*Draco dussumieri*). Tell the
distribution of other species, *Draco norvilli*:
(a) Assam Hill areas (b) Rajasthan desert
(c) Andaman & Nicobar Islands (d) Satpura Hills

779. Which lizard provides an example of the
Malayan affinity in the fauna of south-west
India?
(a) Flying Lizard (*Draco dussumieri*) (b) Spiny-
tailed Lizard (*Uromastyx hardwickii*) (c) Fanthroated Lizard (*Sitana ponticeriana*) (d) No such
example available

780. Name the largest lizard in India which is the
second largest living lizard in the world, next
only to the Komodo Dragon or Ora (*Varanus
komodoensis*) of the Indonesian island of
Komodo:
(a) Common Indian Monitor (*Varanus bengalensis*)
(b) Desert Monitor (*Varanus griseus*) (c) Yellow
Monitor (*Varanus flavescens*) (d) Water Monitor
(*Varanus salvator*)

781. Is it true that all Monitor lizards (*Varanus sp.*) are
endangered by skin trade and have been
included in Schedule 1 of the Wildlife
Protection Act, 1972?
(a) Yes (b) No

782. Desert Monitor (*Varanus griseus*) can be distinguished from all other Monitor lizards of India with the help of tail only . How?
(a) Tail of the Desert Monitor is rounded (b) Desert Monitor has no tail (c) Desert Monitor has very short tail (d) Desert Monitor has two tails

783. Is it true that Monitor lizards (*Varanus sp.*) were used to scale walls and rocks, for once Monitor holds rock surface it is difficult to pull it out?
(a) Yes (b) No

784. What purpose does a snake tongue serve?
(a) Sense organ for taste (b) Sense organ for smell (c) Sense organ for hearing (d) Not known

785. Is it true that snake tongue is forked?
(a) Yes (b) No

786. What purpose venom serves for snakes?
(a) Digestive aid (b) Defence (c) No special purpose (d) Not known

787. What is the chief chemical constituent of the snake venom?
(a) Carbohydrate (b) Protein (c) Minerals (d) Vitamins

788. What are the local symptoms of poisonous snake bite?
(a) Pain (b) Immediate swelling (c) Blisters and necrosis (d) All the above

789. Is it true that swelling of the affected part of the body may not occur in the case of Krait (*Bungarus sp*) bite?
(a) Yes (b) No

790. Is it true that discolouration of the skin around the bite occurs both in the case of Cobra (*Naja*

naja and *Ophiophagus hannah*) and Viper (*Vipera sp*) bites?
(a) Yes (b) No

791. If severe abdominal pain is noticed in the victim of a snake bite, which is the probable snake associated with bite?
(a) Krait (b) King Cobra (c) Cobra (d) Viper

792. What are the most important symptoms of the Viper (*Vipera russelli*) bite in human beings?
(a) Burning and stinging pain at the bite point (b) Local swelling (c) Constant bleeding from the bite point (d) All above

793. What is the first aid to a victim of snake bite?
(a) Bite point should be wiped with clean water and covered by clean bandage (b) Application of a firm ligature above the bite point with a cloth or bandage (c) Shift the patient to the nearest hospital (d) All above

794. What is the longest recorded length of the Indian Python (*Python molurus*) in India?
(a) 5.85 m (b) 6 m (c) 6.2 m (d) 6.4 m

795. Is Indian Python (*Python molurus*) a poisonous snake?
(a) Yes (b) No

796. What is the largest recorded clutch size of the Indian Python (*Python molurus*)?
(a) 100 eggs (b) 107 eggs (c) 120 eggs (d) 150 eggs

797. Which is the longest snake in the world?
(a) Indian Python (*Python molurus*)
(b) Reticulated Python (*Python reticulatus*) (c) King Cobra (*Ophiophagus hannah*) (d) Indian Cobra (*Naja naja*)

798. Which is the longest venomous snake in the world which also occurs in India?
(a) Indian Python (*Python molurus*)
(b) Reticulated Python (*Python reticulatus*) (c) King Cobra (*Ophiophagus hannah*) (d) Indian Cobra (*Naja Naja*)

799. Name the only snake in the world that builds nest. It is found in India also:
(a) Indian Python (*Python molurus*)
(b) Reticulated Python (*Python reticulatus*)
(c) King Cobra (*Ophiophagus hannah*) (d) Indian Cobra (*Naja naja*)

800. Is King Cobra (*Ophiophagus hannah*) also known as Hamadryad?
(a) Yes (b) No

801. How many species of Flying Snakes are found in India?
(a) 2 (b) 4 (c) 6 (d) 8

802. Two species of flying snakes are found in India. The better known species is Golden Tree or Flying Snake (*Chrysopelia ornata*) found in Western Ghats, North-eastern India and Andamans. Which is the other species?
(a) *Chrysopelia paradisi* (b) *Lycodon aulicus*
(c) *Lycodon striatus* (d) *Dendrelphis pictus*

803. What is the distribution of the *Chrysopelea paradisi*—a flying snake?
(a) Narcondam Island (b) Kerala (c) Rajasthan (d) Madhya Pradesh

804. Which harmless snake in India is mistaken for Cobra (*Naja naja*)?
(a) Rat Snake (*Elaphe obsoleta*) (b) Common Kukri Snake (*Oligodon arnensis*) (c) Common

Wolf Snake (*Lycodon aulicus*) (d) None of the above

805. Which snake produces the costliest venom in India? It could fetch more than Rs. 1000 per gram.
(a) Common Indian Krait (*Bungarus caeruleus*)
(b) Banded Krait (*B. fasciatus*) (c) Indian Cobra (*Naja naja*) (d) (a) and (b) both

806. What is the more popular name of the Golden Tree Snake (*Chrysopelia Ornata*)?
(a) Cobra (b) Krait (c) Flying Snake (d) Flat Tail

807. Which poisonous snake has alternating yellow and black bands?
(a) Common Indian Krait (*Bungarus caeruleus*)
(b) Reticulated Python (*Python reticulates*)
(c) Banded Krait (*Bungarus asiaticus*)
(d) Yellowbanded Wolf Snake (*Lycodon fasciatus*)

808. Which non-poisonous snake resembles the Banded Krait (*Bungarus fasciatus*)?
(a) Common Indian Krait (*Bungarus caeruleus*)
(b) Reticulated Python (*Python reticulatus*) (c) Banded Krait (*Bungarus asiaticus*)
(d) Yellowbanded Wolf Snake (*Lycodon fasciatus*)

809. Are Banded Krait (*Bungarus fasciatus*) and the Common Indian Krait (*B. caeruleus*) venomous snakes?
(a) Yes (b) No

810. Of the 16 species of Pythons in the world, how many are found in India?
(a) 2 (b) 4 (c) 6 (d) 8

811. Is it true that Indian Egg-eater Snake (*Elachiston westermanni*) is known from a few female specimens and the male is yet to be found?

(a) Yes (b) No

812. Is it true that the Indian Egg-eater Snake (*Elachiston westermanni*) shows the morphological and ethological affinity to African Egg-eater Snake and is one of the rarest snakes of India. It feeds exclusively on bird eggs which are swallowed up whole.
(a) Yes (b) No

9

THE AMPHIBIANS

813. Which is the most beautiful living Indian amphibian based on the colour pattern on the body?
(a) Ceylon Kaloula (b) Malay Bull Frog (c) *Kaloula pulchra taprobanica* (d) (a) (b) (c) refer to same frog

814. Are amphibians cold blooded animals?
(a) Yes (b) No

815. All the three orders of amphibia are represented in India. What is the number of species found in India?
(a) 142 (b) 152 (c) 162 (d) 172

816. Which is the largest Indian frog?
(a) Indian Bull Frog (*Rana tigrina*) (b) Ceylon Bull Frog (*Kaloula pulchra*) (c) *Nannobatrachus beddomii* (d) None of the above

817. Which is the smallest Indian frog?

(a) Indian Bull Frog (*Rana tigrina*) (b) Ceylon Bull Frog (*Kaloula pulchra*) (c) *Nannobatrachus beddomii* (d) None of the above

818. Is it true that the Indian Newt (*Tylototriton verrucosus*) found in North-east India is the only representative of the tailed amphibia in India?
(a) Yes (b) No

819. Is it true that the Indian Newt (*Tylototriton verrucosus*) is the only species of Salamander known from India?
(a) Yes (b) No

820. Which biogeographic zone of India has the maximum number of endemic amphibian genera in India?
(a) North-east India (b) Eastern India (c) Western Ghats (d) Indo-Gangetic Plain

821. Name the frog found in the Kerala and the Karnataka forests which is sometimes referred as Indian counterpart of the Malayan Flying Frog:
(a) Tree Frog (*Rhaccophorus reinwardtii*)
(b) Variable Ramanella (*Ramanella variegata*)
(c) Indian Bull Frog (*Rana tigrina*) (d) Ceylon Keloula (*Kaloula pulchra*)

822. Is it true that the Tree Frog (*Rhaccophorus reinwardtii malabaricus*) uses webbed feet for gliding from tree top to the ground?
(a) Yes (b) No

823. Which frog often occurs in association with the black scorpion (*Heterometrus sp.*)?
(a) Tree Frog (*Rhaccophorus reinwardtii*)
(b) Variable Ramanella (*Ramanella variegata*)
(c) Malay Bull Frog (*Kaloula pulchra*) (d) None of the above

824. Is it true that Malabar Tree Toad (*Pedostibes tuberculosus*) was found in Kerala about a century ago, and not seen subsequently. Recently it has been spotted and collected from the Silent Valley National Park and Ponmudi forests of Kerala.
(a) Yes (b) No

825. Name the amphibian listed in Schedule 1 of the Wildlife Protection Act, 1972:
(a) Himalayan Newt (*Tylototriton verrucosus*) (b) Tree Frog (*Raccophorus reinwardtii*) (c) Malay Bull Frog (*Kaloula pulchra*) (d) No amphibian listed in Schedule 1

826. What does the word Amphibia mean?
(a) Animals living in water (b) Animals living on land (c) Animals adapted to land and water (d) Animals having cold blood

10

FISHES AND OTHER CREATURES

827. Which is the largest fish in India?
(a) Whale Shark (*Rhineodon typus*) (b) Stone Fish (*Synanceia horrida*) (c) Striped Marlin (*Tetrapturus brevirostris*) (d) Hilsa (*Hilsa hilsa*)

828. Which is the most venomous fish in the world that is found in India too?
(a) Whale Shark (*Rhineodon typus*) (b) Stone Fish (*Synanceia horrida*) (c) Striped Marlin (*Tetrapturus brevirostris*) (d) Hilsa (*Hilsa hilsa*)

829. Which Indian fish often attacks the boats with its snout?
(a) Whale Shark (*Rhineodon typus*) (b) Stone Fish (*Synanceia horrida*) (c) Striped Marlin (*Tetrapturus brevirostris*) (d) Hilsa (*Hilsa hilsa*)

830. Name a fish found on the west coast of India which cleans the mouth of other fish to eat parasites. It is the process of procuring food:
(a) Stone Fish (b) Doctor Fish (c) Whale Shark (d) Hilsa

831. Is it true that Bombay Duck is a fish zoologically known as *Harpodon nehereus?*
(a) Yes (b) No

832. Which is the only Indian anadromous (which migrates from sea up the river) fish?
(a) Hilsa (*Hilsa hilsa*) (b) Climbing Perch (*Ananbas testudineus*) (c) Bombay Duck (*Harpodon nehereus*) (d) Striped Marlin (*Tetrapturus brevirostris*)

833. Which fish in India can remain out of water and move long distances on the land?
(a) Hilsa (*Hilsa hilsa*) (b) Climbing Perch (*Ananbas testudineus*) (c) Bombay Duck (*Harpodon nehereus*) (d) Striped Marlin (*Tetrapturus brevirostris*)

834. Which fish is used as a decoy to trap dolphins (*Delphinus sp.)?*
(a) Hilsa (*Hilsa hilsa*) (b) Climbing Perch (*Ananbas testudineus*) (c) Bombay Duck (*Harpodon nehereus*) (d) Striped Marlin (*Tetrapturus brevirostris*)

835. How many species of venomous marine fishes are found in Indian waters?
(a) 32 (b) 50 (c) 100 (d) 107

836. How many species of poisonous fishes are found in Indian waters?

(a) 56 (b) 60 (c) 69 (d) 75

837. Is it true that a butterfly *Mycalesis rama* occurs only in Sri Lankan bamboo forests of Ratnapura and Kottawa. It was suggested by R.K. Varshney to introduce it into the bamboo forests of Kerala?
(a) Yes (b) No

838. Name the largest crab in the world. It is found in India too:
(a) Robber Crab (*Birgus latro*) (b) Coconut Crab
(c) (a) & (b) are synonymous

839. Is it true that Mulberry Silk Worm from which raw silk is obtained no longer exists in the wild?
(a) Yes (b) No

840. Name the largest known moth which occurs in India too:
(a) Atlas Moth (*Attacus atlas*) (b) Silk Moth (*Bombyx mori*) (c) *Mycalesis rama* (d) None of the above

841. Is it true that *Heletrometrus swammerdami* is the largest scorpion in the world and it occurs in India too?
(a) Yes (b) No

11

PLANTS, FORESTS AND HABITAT

842. The most interesting feature of the high level forests of the Nilgiris is their affinity to the

forests of a distant hill range in India. Which hill range?

(a) Assam   (b) Eastern Ghats   (c) Satpura (d) Vindhyas

843. It is an endangered endemic tree occurring in an small area in Andhra Pradesh. Scarlet-purple coloured heartwood contains a dye. Timber with wavy grain fetches a fancy price. Identify it:

(a) Chandan (*Santalum album*) (b) Red Sanders (*Pterocarpus santalinus*) (c) Bija (*P. marsupium*) (d) Teak (*Tectona grandis*)

844. Which tree yields a dye called Santolin?

(a) Chandan (*Santalum album*) (b) Red Sanders (*Pterocarpus santalinus*) (c) Bija (*P. marsupium*) (d) Teak (*Tectona grandis*)

845. Name the most valuable tree of forestry importance which is also an example of partial root parasite?

(a) Sandal (*Santalum album*) (b) Sal (*Shorea robusta*) (c) Khair (*Acacia catechu*) (d) Chir Pine (*Pinus roxburghi*)

846. What for the Upas tree (*Antiaris toxicaria*) is used?

(a) Arrow-poisoning by tribals (b) Food during drought (c) Fodder for cattle (d) No use

847. What is the dominant flora of alpine Himalayas?

(a) Pines (b) Rhododendrons (c) Deodar (d) Teak

848. Rhododendrons are found in the alpine zone of Himalayas. Western Himalayas has only 5

species of *Rhododendron*. How many species are found in the Eastern Himalayas?

(a) 10 (b) 30 (c) 50 (d) 80

849. Name a rare showy ephiphyte species of Rhododendron reported to have been collected only on three occasions during the last hundred years:

(a) *Rhododendron campanulatum* (b) *R. nilaghirica* (c) *R. edgeworythii* (d) *R. alba*

850. A tree considered to have become extinct many centuries ago was discovered in 1941 in China. This discovery aroused interest throughout the world for propagation of the species. There are few trees growing in Darjeeling and Almora. Name this fossil tree:

(a) Maidenhair Tree (*Ginkgo biloba*) (b) Dawn Redwood (*Metasequoia glyptostroboides*) (c) Giant Sequoia (*Sequoiadendron giganteum*) (d) Chilgoza (*Pinus gerardiana*)

851. Name a wild flowering plant threatened with extinction which was discovered in Mishmi hills in the year 1836. It has only been sighted twice since its discovery. The plant is a stemless and leafless root parasite of *Vitis sp*. Deep crimson coloured flowers are about 35 cm in diameter:

(a) Sapria (*Sapria himalayana*) (b) Vits (*Vitis himalayana*) (c) Sandal (*Santalum album*) (d) Red Sanders (*Pterocarpus santalinus*)

852. Which Rhododendron grows at the highest altitude in the Indian Himalayas?

(a) *Rhododendron nivale* (b) *R. arboreum* (c) *R. campanulatum* (d) *R. alba*

853. What is the height of the dwarf Rhododendron (*Rhododendron nivale*)?
(a) 1 cm (b) 5 cm (c) 10 cm (d) 20 cm

854. How many species of plants are found in India?
(a) 45,000 (b) 50,000 (c) 60,000 (d) 70,000

855. How many species of vascular plants are found in India?
(a) 15,000 (b) 25,000 (c) 30,000 (d) 40,000

856. It is feared that many species of vascular plants may fall in one or the other category of threatened species in India? How many are threatened currently?
(a) 1,000 (b) 2,000 (c) 3,000 (d) 4,000

857. Is it true that about 5 per cent of all recorded plant and animal species on earth are found in India?
(a) Yes (b) No

858. What is an endemic taxa of plants?
(a) Taxa growing in a specific area only (b) Taxa growing throughout the globe (c) Taxa growing in the mountains (d) Taxa growing in the seas

859. What percentage of vascular plants in India is endemic?
(a) 10 (b) 20 (c) 35 (d) 55

860. Which endemic plant from Andaman and Nicobar Islands has been named after the Father of Indian ethnobotany, Dr. S.K. Jain?
(a) *Jainia nicobarica* (b) *Jainia andamanica* (c) *Nicobarica jainii* (d) *Andamanica jainii*

861. Of the 450 species of carnivorous plants in the world, how many are found in the Indian sub-continent?

(a) 40 (b) 50 (c) 60 (d) 70

862. Pitcher plants are the most remarkable of insectivorous plants found in India. We have only one species, *Nepenthes khasiana*. What is the distribution of the species?
(a) Khasi Hills (b) Jaintia Hills (c) Garo Hills (d) All the above

863. What is the *in situ* conservation method?
(a) Protection of natural habitat of the plant species (b) Management of bio-diversity by plantation (c) Growing of rare plants through tissue culture (d) All the above

864. Name the plant which is threatened with extinction for it has so far been recorded growing only inside the compound of a bungalow in Dehra Dun:
(a) *Jainia nicobarica* (b) *J. andamanica* (c) *Peucedanum dehradunensis* (d) No such plant exists

865. Which plant in India produces the largest inflorescence in the world?
(a) Talipot Palm (*Corypha umbraculifera*) (b) Toddy Palm (*Caryota urens*) (c) Branching Palm (*Hyphaene dichotoma*) (d) Tree is not found in India

866. Tropics of which continent possess the richest diversity of palms in the world?
(a) Africa (b) Asia (c) South America (d) Australia

867. Name an endemic palm growing gregariously in the coastal sands of the Diu Island in India. Peculiarity of the Palm is its dichotomous branching:

(a) Branching Palm (*Hyphaene dichotoma*)
(b) Talipot palm (*Corypha umbraculifera*)
(c) Palmyra Palm (*Borassus falbellifer*) (d) Areca
Palm (*Areca catechu*)

868. Name the only conifer occurring wild in
peninsular India?
(a) Spruce (*Picea smithiana*) (b) Silver Fir (*Abies pindrow*) (c) *Decussocarpus wallichianus* (d) Deodar
(*Cedrus deodara*)

869. Which of the following is a Chilgoza Pine?
(a) *Pinus roxburghii* (b) *Pinus wallichiana* (c) *Pinus gerardiana* (d) *Pinus khasya*

870. Is it true that Chilgoza Pine (*Pinus gerardiana*) is
an endemic tree of Western Himalayas and
yields the Chilgoza seeds of commerce?
(a) Yes (b) No

871. Name the State Tree of Tamil Nadu:
(a) Branching Palm (*Hyphaene dichotoma*)
(b) Talipot Palm (*Corypha umbraculifera*)
(c) Palmyra Palm (*Borassus falbellifer*) (d) Areca
Palm (*Areca catechu*)

872. Which grass was utilized to obtain the resistant
variety of sugarcane against the Red-rot?
(a) *Saccharum spontaneum* (b) *Saccharum munja*
(c) *Cyanodon dactylon* (d) *Dicanthium annulatum*

873. Indian forests and tribal farming areas hold the
rich biodiversity in the paddy gene resources.
What is the number of traditional land races of
wild rice in India as per the estimates of the
year 1950?
(a) 30,000 (b) 20,000 (c) 10,000 (d) 400

874. The great civilizations of the world utilized
cereals as the main source of food. Civilizations

of the Mesopotamia, Egypt, Greece and Rome were thriving on wheat. Maize was the basis for the Inca, Aztec and Mayan empires in Americas. What was the staple food in India, China and Japan?

(a) Rice (b) Wheat (c) Gram (d) Not known

875. Name the bamboo in India that produces large fleshy fruits, nearly the size of guavas. Fruits are important ethnobotanical food resource of tribals:

(a) Muli Bamboo (b) *Melocana baccifera*
(c) *Melocana bambusoides* (d) All above are same

876. What is the *vivipary* in the plants?

(a) Germination of seeds while the fruit is still attached to the mother plant. (b) Non-flowering of plant (c) Non-fruiting of plant (d) None of the above

877. Which bamboo in India shows viviparous germination?

(a) Muli Bamboo (*Melocana bambusoides Syn. M. baccifera*) (b) Solid Bamboo (*Dendrocalamus strictus*) (c) Golden Bamboo (*Bambusa vulgaris*)

878. Identify the world's smallest flowering plant, occurring on freshwater tanks and ponds:

(a) *Wolffia arrhiza* (b) *Ermania himalayensis*
(c) *Trichodesmium erythrium* (d) *Adamsonia digitata*

879. Is it true that Baobab tree (*Adamsonia digitata*) with bottle-shaped huge trunk is reported to possess the property of preserving human corpses?

(a) Yes (b) No

880. Is it true that Baobab tree (*Adamsonia digitata*) is an exotic to India brought from Africa by Arabs?
(a) Yes (b) No

881. Which algae is responsible for large scale bloom along the west coast?
(a) *Trichodesmium erythrium* (b) *Micromonas pusilla* (c) *Monas stigmata* (d) Not known

882. What is the reason for the ascent of tree line in the Eastern Himalayas in comparison to the Western Himalayas?
(a) Rich soil (b) Higher humidity and rainfall (c) Latitude variation (d) Longitude variation

883. Why is there a need for constant infusion of wild genes in the cultivated species?
(a) To maintain the genetic diversity of cultivated plants (b) To increase disease resistance in cultivars (c) No specific reason (d) (a) & (b) both

884. Which fungi is collected by the local people from the wildlands of the Himalayas, fetching a high price in the local market?
(a) *Morchella esculenta* (b) *Amanita muscaria* (c) *Rhizopus stolonifer* (d) Not known

885. People of which tribe in Kerala cure their urinary disorders by the seeds of Wild Banana?
(a) Kol (b) Irula (c) Kadar (d) Kuriche

886. How many parent plants were used initially to breed the cultivated varieties of rice for Asia by the International Rice Research Institute, Manila?
(a) 11 (b) 15 (c) 20 (d) 41

887. Wild growing stock of which tree are being greatly threatened in India?
(a) Sandal (*Santalum album*), (b) Red Sanders (*Pterocarpus santalinus*) (c) (a) & (b) both (d) No such threat to any tree in India

888. As per the World Conservation Strategy, how fertile lands can be managed properly?
(a) By soil and water conservation (b) Recycling nutrients by returning crop residues and livestock wastes to the land (c) Retaining the habitats or organisms beneficial to agriculture (d) All above

889. Name the tallest recorded Bamboo in the world. It was felled at Pattazhi in Kerala in the year 1904 and measured 121 ft 6 in:
(a) Thorny Bamboo (*Bambusa arundinacea*) (b) Golden Bamboo (*B. vulgaris*) (c) Solid Bamboo (*Dendrocalamus strictus*) (d) Muli Bamboo (*Melocana bambusoides*)

890. Name the State Tree of Madhya Pradesh?
(a) Sandal (*Santalum album*) (b) Mango (*Mangifera indica*) (c) Peepal (*Ficus religiosa*) (d) Banyan (*Ficus bengalensis*)

891. Is *Glutea travencoria*, a dye-yielding tree, endemic to South India?
(a) Yes (b) No

892. Who classified the forests of India systematically in his book, *The Forest Types of India*?
(a) D. Brandis (b) N. L. Bor & M. B. Raizada (c) Champion & Seth (d) J. D. Hooker

893. Is it true that Teak (*Tectona grandis*) forests are mostly distributed in Central and peninsular India?
(a) Yes (b) No

894. Is it true that Sal (*Shorea robusta*) forests are mostly distributed in the North and North-eastern India?
(a) Yes (b) No

895. Name the sanctuary created to guard against the gene-pool erosion of the wild races of *Citrus*.
(a) Tura Ridge, Meghalaya (b) Khursel, M.P.
(c) Kanger, M.P. (d) Perambiculum, Kerala

12

WILDLIFE AND GENETIC RESOURCE

896. Name the tree which was depleted in its natural habitat in South America and seeds had to be propagated at Kew to help establish this tree in India. It yields an effective drug against malaria:
(a) *Chinchona sp* (b) *Coffee arabica* (c) *Penicillium notatum* (d) *Erythroxylon coca*

897. From which fungus you get pencillin?
(a) *Chinchona sp* (b) *Coffee arabica* (c) *Penicillium notatum* (d) *Erythroxylon coca*

898. From which plant is *cocaine* extracted?
(a) *Chinchona sp* (b) *Coffee arabica* (c) *Penicillium notatum* (d) *Erythroxylon coca*

899. Which tree in Mauritius stopped propagation supposedly due to Dodo's extinction, as seeds

of the tree could germinate only when passed through the intestine of the Dodo (*Raphus cucullatus*)?

(a) *Calvaria major* (b) *Santalum albumu* (c) *Alstonia constricta* (d) None of the above

900. Name the Cactus which is utilized by the woodpecker to excavate nests and when deserted, Red Indians of South-west USA use it as water bottle:

(a) Saguaro cactus (*Cereus giganteus*) (b) Golden barrel cactus (*Echinocactus grusonii*) (c) Thornless cactus (*Nopalia cochinilifera*) (d) Opuntia (*Opuntia dillenii*)

901. Which fungus is most widely utilized in alcohol preparation?

(a) Yeast (b) Morchella (c) Mucor (d) Amanita

902. Which tree yields natural chewing gum?

(a) Chile Tree (*Manilkara zapota*) (b) Neem (*Azadirachta indica*) (c) Katira (*Sterculia urens*) (d) Bija (*Pterocarpus marsupium*)

903. What commercial product is obtained from the Quebracho (*Aspidosperma quebracho*)?

(a) Tannin (b) Food (c) Fuelwood (d) Dye

904. Modern wheat hybrids have an ancestry to the Wild Einkorn (*Triticum boeticum*) and a wild grass which you have to name:

(a) *Triticum vulgare* (b) *Hordeum vulgare* (c) *Sehima nervosum* (d) *Aegilops speltoides*

905. For the species known from a single growing plant, artificial regeneration is the only answer to save it from extinction. Name a species known from a single specimen growing in Rodrigues. Its cuttings were taken to Kew

Royal Botanical Garden and successfully regenerated:
(a) Cafe Marron (*Ramosmania heterophylla*)
(b) Tambalacoque (*Calvaria major*) (c) Red Wood (*Trochetiopsis erythroxylon*) (d) White Pine (*Pinus strobus*)

906. Which of the following trees are depleted in the wild as a result of logging and habitat destruction?
(a) Red Cedar (*Toona australis*), Australia
(b) White Pine (*Pinus strobus*), North America
(c) Chinese Coffinwood (*Taiwania cryptomerioides*) (d) Fir (*Abies nebrodensis*), Sicily
(e) All above

907. Which Asian country became the first in the world in 1980 to establish a ministry for indigenous medicines and medicinal plants?
(a) India (b) Nepal (c) Sri Lanka (d) Bhutan

908. When in the year 1982, U.N. agencies tried to draft a "Plan of action for the wise management of tropical forests", the attempt failed because of non-participation of Brazil, Zaire, Colombia and
(a) Venezuela (b) Peru (c) Sudan (d) India

909. Which is the world's richest biological region?
(a) Tropical Moist Forests (b) Tropical Dry Forests (c) Coniferous Forests (d) Wetlands

910. The aborigines of the African tropical moist forests were Bushmen and Hottentots. A large number of Pygmies still live in the African tropical moist forests. Where are Bushmen living?

(a) Kalahari Desert (b) Sahara Desert (c) Gobi Desert (d) Thar Desert

911. What do you mean by *commercial extinction* of a species?
(a) Non-availability of the species in the wild due to over-exploitation (b) Species totally wiped off from the natural habitat (c) Ban on commercial exploitation of species (d) None of the above

912. Is it true that coffee plantations in Brazil derived from a single variety were damaged due to leaf rust attack and African forests had to supply the wild genetic resource to breed a new resistant variety?
(a) Yes (b) No

913. Is it true that 85 per cent of the world's food supply comes from only eight species of plants?
(a) Yes (b) No

914. Which of the following plant yields the golden fruit of the Andes?
(a) Naranjilla (*Solanum quitoense*) (b) Wax Gourd (*Benincasa hispida*) (c) Taro (*Colocasia esculenta*) (d) Wild Rice (*Oryza mauritiana*)

915. Which of the following ethnobotanical trees of Amazon forests are potential source of oil?
(a) *Jessenia polycarpa* (b) Babassu Palm (*Orbignya sp.*) (c) Copaifera Diesel tree (d) All above

916. Without the discovery of which plant it would not have been possible to produce the birth control pills?
(a) Mexican Yam (*Dioscorea composita*) (b) Green Heart Tree (*Nectandra rodiaei*) (c) Coca

(*Erythroxylum coca*) (d) Ginseng (*Panaxia quinquefolia*)

917. During the ice-sheeted Pleistocene some areas escaped from being covered by ice and acted as habitat islands isolated from one another for long times during which new species originated. What are these habitat islands called?

(a) *Pleistocene refugium* (b) Pleistocene islands (c) Pleistocene shelters (d) No specific name

918. What is the characteristic of the *Pleistocene refugia?*

(a) Centre of high biotic diversity (b) Few species per unit area (c) No economic genetic resource available (d) None of the above

919. In the year 1981, the International Board for Plant Genetic Resources prepared the list of priority regions for the conservation of crop genetic resources and land races. In which priority area does India fall?

(a) Priority I (b) Priority II (c) Priority III (d) Not included in the list

920. Which of the following wild plants were drawn from India to improve the major world crops?

(a) Rice (Wild Rice—*Oryza nivara*) (b) Sesame (Wild Sesame—*Sesame orientale malabaricum*) (c) Sugarcane (Wild grass—*Saccharum spontaneum*) (d) All above

921. In the year 1966, Dr. S.D. Sharma collected a single sample of wild rice from central India. It helped to breed for the *cultivar* which now has

resistance to *blast* and *grassy stunt virus*. Name the wild species:

(a) *Oryza nivara* (b) *O. sativa* (c) *O. mauritiana* (d) *O. rufipogon*

922. What is the South Africa's National Flower?

(a) *Protea repens* (b) *Brosimum utile* (c) *Puya raimondii* (d) *Adiandra dumosa*

923. South American Milk Tree produces a sap which is used as milk by Venezuelans. What is the scientific name of the tree?

(a) *Protea repens* (b) *Brosimum utile* (c) *Puya raimondii* (d) *Adiandra dumosa*

924. Which species of bamboo is a favourite food of Giant Panda (*Ailuropoda melanoleuca*)?

(a) *Sinarundinacea fangiana* (b) *Bambusa vulgaris* (c) *Dendrocalamus strictus* (d) *Bambusa tulda*

925. Name the fastest growing fungus in the world which is found in tropical Brazil:

(a) Stink horn Fungus (*Dictyophora sp.*) (b) Fly Agaric (*Amanita muscaria*) (c) Guchhi (*Morchella esculenta* (d) Not known

926. In the year 1954 the oldest known living seed was found in frozen silt in Canada. Its age was estimated to be 10,000 years. To which species does the seed belong?

(a) Arctic Lupin (*Lupinus arcticus*) (b) Giant Water Lily (*Victoria azazonica*) (c) Pitcher Plant (*Nepenthes rajah*) (d) Pummelo (*Citrus maxima*)

927. Which is the biggest pitcher plant having a capacity of 2 litres to trap the insects?

(a) *Nepenthes khasiana* (b) *Nepenthes rajah* (c) *Nepenthes alba* (d) None of the above

928. Which country has the maximum number of orchids in the world?
(a) Colombia (b) Bhutan (c) India (d) Canada

929. Which is the longest palm on earth?
(a) Rattan Palm (b) Wax Palm (*Ceroxylon quinuense*) (c) Coconut (*Cocos nucifera*) (d) Palmyra Palm (*Borassus flabellifer*)

930. Which is the largest cactus in the world?
(a) Saguaro (*Cereus giganteus*) (b) Golden Barrel Cactus (*Echinocactus grusonii*) (c) Thornless Cactus (*Nopalia cochinilifera*) (d) Opnutia (*Opnutia dillenii*)

931. Which is the heaviest wood in the world?
(a) Black Iron Wood (*Olea lauritolia*) (b) Balsa Tree (*Ochroma pyramidale*) (c) Durian (*Durio zibethinus*) (d) Coco de Mer (*Lodoicea maldivica*)

932. Which is the largest seed in the plant
(a) Black Iron Wood (*Olea lauritolia*) (b) Balsa Tree (*Ochroma pyramidale*) (c) Durian (*Durio zibethinus*) (d) Coco de Mer (*Lodoicea maldivica*)

933. Fruits of which South-west Asian tree are rated as most delicious in the world?
(a) Black Iron Wood (*Olea lauritolia*) (b) Balsa Tree (*Ochroma pyramidale*) (c) Durian (*Durio zibethinus*) (d) Coco de Mer (*Lodoicea maldivica*)

934. The National Tree of Colombia is the tallest palm on earth growing up to 60 m. A separate protected area, Al Quindio Reserve, was established to accord protection. Name the palm:
(a) Toddy Palm (*Caryota urens*) (b) Wax Palm (*Ceroxylon quinuense*) (c) Palmyra Palm (*Borassus flabellifer*) (d) Coconut (*Cocos nucifera*)

935. Name the parasitic plant named after the founder of Singapore, Sir Stamford Raffles. It is the largest and perhaps the smelliest flower in the world:

(a) Rafflesia (*Rafflesia arnoldii*) (b) Ceropegia (*Ceropegia haygarthii*) (c) Giant Water Lily (*Victoria amazonica*) (d) Kapok (*Ceiba pentandra*)

936. Which is the oldest tree on earth alive today?

(a) Giant Sequoia (*Sequoiadendron giganteum*)
(b) Coast Redwood (*Sequoia sempervirens*)
(c) Montezuma Cypress (*Taxodium mucronatum*)
(d) Bristle Cone Pine (*Pinus aristata Syn. Pinus longaeva*)

937. Which is the most massive tree in the world?

(a) Giant Sequoia (*Sequoiadendron giganteum*)
(b) Coast Redwood (*Sequoia sempervirens*)
(c) Montezuma Cypress (*Taxodium mucronatum*)
(d) Bristle Cone Pine (*Pinus aristata Syn. Pinus longaeva*)

938. Which is the tallest tree in the world?

(a) Giant Sequoia (*Sequoiadendron giganteum*)
(b) Coast Redwood (*Sequoia sempervirens*)
(c) Montezuma Cypress (*Taxodium mucronatum*)
(d) Bristle Cone Pine (*Pinus aristata Syn. Pinus longaeva*)

939. Which tree has the maximum girth in the world?

(a) Giant Sequoia (*Sequoiadendron giganteum*)
(b) Coast Redwood (*Sequoia sempervirens*)
(c) Montezuma Cypress (*Taxodium mucronatum*)
(d) Bristle Cone Pine (*Pinus aristata Syn. Pinus longaeva*)

940. In which country is the famous wetland, the Shinhama Reserve, located?
(a) India (b) Japan (c) China (d) Bhutan

941. Name the largest wetland nature reserve o China that holds the largest breeding population of the Redcrowned Crane (*Gru japonensis*) left in the world?
(a) Zhalong Reserve (b) Shinhama Reserve (c) Jilin Reserve (d) None of the above

942. Which are the world's largest forests in area?
(a) Coniferous Forests in Siberia (b) Rain Forests in Amazonia (c) Dry Deciduous Forests in India (d) Moist Deciduous Forests in India

943. For what kind of forests is Amazonia famous?
(a) Coniferous forests (b) Rain forests (c) Deciduous forests (d) Bamboo forests

944. Name the place where rivers contain 40 per cent of all the world's species of freshwater fish and 319 forms of humming birds:
(a) Amazonia (b) Siberia (c) Andaman & Nicobar Islands (d) Oceania

945. Bhutan stands across the two zoogeographical regions of the world. One is the Oriental region. Which is the other?
(a) Palearctic (b) Nearctic (c) Neotropical (d) Afrotropical

946. Name the fish which was thought to be extinct 70 million years ago; it was rediscovered in the year 1938 off the mouth of Chalumna river:
(a) Coelacanth (*Latimeria chalumnae*) (b) Pla Buk (*Pangasianodon gigas*) (c) White Shark (*Carcharodon carcharius*) (d) Dwarf Gobi (*Trimmatom nanus*)

947. Largest scorpion of the world is found in India. Name it:

(a) *Heterometrus swammerdami* (b) *Leiurus quinquestriatus* (c) *Microbothus pusillus* (d) *Theraphosa blondi*

948. Is it true that larvae of the Californian Petroleum Fly (*Psilopa petrolei*) lives in pools of crude oil near the oilfields?

(a) Yes (b) No

949. In which European country the bird Osprey (*Pandion haliaectus*) became near extinct and Operation Osprey was started for its conservation?

(a) Scotland (b) India (c) Peru (d) Eucador

950. Which is the world's largest private international nature conservation organization with 3 million supporters and currently 27 affiliate and associate organizations on five continents?

(a) World Wide Fund for Nature (b) International Union for Conservation of Nature and Natural Resources (c) Food and Agriculture Organization (d) Bombay Natural History Society

951. Name the famous painter whose bird paintings of Florida Everglades fetch mind-boggling price in the market:

(a) John H. Dick (b) John J. Audubon (c) Sir David Attenborough (d) J. P. Irani

952. Name a small carnivore that preys on birds found at the River Tana, Kenya, where famous Whitefaced Tree Ducks are found:

(a) Serval (*Felis serval*) (b) Capybara (*Hydrochoerus hydrochaeris*) (c) Tiger (*Panthera tigris*) (d) (a) & (b) both

953. Is it true that Thylacine or Tasmanian Wolf (*Thylacinus cynocephalus*) is the largest of the carnivorous marsupials? It was once common in Australia but now survives in small numbers in Tasmania:
(a) Yes (b) No

954. Name the animal that looks like a cross between a Zebra and Giraffe. It is found only in the forests of Zaire where the Zaire Institute for Conservation of Nature is putting efforts to protect its last home:
(a) Okapi (*Okapia johnstoni*) (b) Kodiak Bear (*Ursus arctos middendorffi*) (c) Threetoed Sloth (*Bradypus tridaclylus*) (d) Sea Otter (*Enhydra lutris*)

955. Name the only species of bear found south of the equator:
(a) Sloth Bear (*Melursus ursinus*) (b) Spectacled Bear (*Tremarctos ornatus*) (c) Brown Bear (*Ursus arctos*) (d) Himalayan Black Bear (*Selenarctos thibetanus*)

956. It is not possible to assess population of Orang Utan (*Pongo pygmaeus*) by direct visual count. By taking advantage of a unique behaviour of species its distribution and population size has been ascertained by ground and aerial surveys. What is the unique behaviour?
(a) Nest Building (b) Howling (c) Jumping (d) Leaf feeding

957. The world's smallest deer Pudu (*Pudu pudu*) is listed in Schedule I of CITES; what does it mean?

(a) All international trade on this deer is banned (b) Limited trade is allowed (c) Species is extinct (d) No ban on trade

958. There is one species of wild cattle found only in the borders of Kampuchea and its three neighbours, Laos, Thailand and Vietnam. It is considered to carry genes for rinder pest resistance. Name the animal:

(a) Kouprey (*Bos sauveli*) (b) Banteng (*Bos banteng*) (c) Yak (*Bos grunniens*) (d) Gaur (*Bos gaurus*)

959. Which of the following animals you find at Serengati-Mara ecosystem?

(a) Wildebeest (*Connochaetes taurinus*) (b) Zebra (c) (a) & (b) both (d) None of the above

960. In the year 1964, a new cat was discovered. It is said to be the most primitive of the cat family and extremely rare. Give the name of the cat:

(a) Iriomote Wild Cat (*Mayailurus iriomotensis*) (b) Rustyspotted Cat (*Felis rubiginosa*) (c) Jungle Cat (*Felis chaus*) (d) Golden Cat (*Felis temmincki*)

961. Which is the largest monkey in the world?

(a) Mandrill (*Mandrillus sphinx*) (b) Pygmy Marmoset (*Cebuella pygmaea*) (c) Man (*Homo sapiens*) (d) Gorilla (*Gorilla gorilla*)

962. Which is the smallest monkey in the world?

(a) Mandrill (*Mandrillus sphinx*) (b) Pygmy Marmoset (*Cebuella pygmaea*) (c) Man (*Homo sapiens*) (d) Gorilla (*Gorilla gorilla*)

963. Which is the rarest butterfly in the world?

(a) Birdwing Butterfly (*Ornithopteria allottei*)
(b) Alexandra Birdwing Butterfly (*O. alexandrae*) (c) Owlet Moth (*Thysania agrippina*) (d) None of the above

964. In which country is the Central Kalahari Game Reserve situated?
(a) Botswana (b) Bolivia (c) Venezuela (d) Zimbabwe

965. In which country is the Garamba National Park located?
(a) Zaire (b) Botswana (c) Kenya (d) Brazil

966. In which country is the Kora National Reserve located?
(a) Zaire (b) Botswana (c) Kenya (d) Brazil

967. In which country is the Lenin National Park located?
(a) USSR (b) Argentina (c) Zambia (d) Nepal

968. In which country is the Sagarmatha National Park located?
(a) Nepal (b) Bhutan (c) Pakistan (d) Sri Lanka

969. Name the National Bird of the USA?
(a) Bald Eagle (*Haliaeetus leucocephalus*) (b) Osprey (*Pandion haliaetus*) (c) Crested Serpent Eagle (*Spilornis Cheela*) (d) Golden Eagle (*Aquila chrysaetos*)

970. Which bird was the symbol of Rome's power?
(a) Bald Eagle (*Haliaeetus leucocephalus*) (b) Osprey (*Pandion haliaetus*) (c) Crested Serpent Eagle (*Spilornis cheela*) (d) Golden Eagle (*Aquila chrysaetos*)

971. What is the distribution of Penguins in the world?

(a) Southern hemisphere (b) Northern hemisphere (c) Southern and northern hemispheres (d) Both sides of the equator

972. A bird of Madagascar laid a two-gallon-capacity egg which is the largest single animal cell known. Name the bird which is now extinct:
(a) Elephant Bird (*Aepyornis maximus*) (b) Giant Moa (*Dinornis maximus*) (c) Huia (*Heteralocha acutirostris*) (d) Solitaire (*Raphus solitarius*)

973. The Giant Moa (*Dinornis maximus*) is an extinct bird. In which country was it found?
(a) New Zealand (b) Australia (c) Nepal (d) India

974. The Huia (*Heteralocha acutirostris*), a bird of New Zealand, became extinct in the early years of present century. It was last sighted in the year 1907. What was the chief reason of extinction?
(a) Feather trade (b) Natural predation (c) Racial senescence (d) Not known

975. Name the country which has the maximum number of species of Cranes in the world?
(a) China, 8 species (b) India, 6 species (c) Japan, 11 species (d) Nepal, 9 species

976. Name the Parrot of the North America which had the habit of returning to try to help the dead or wounded flockmates. This made them to be shot easily and thus the bird became extinct?
(a) Mauritius Parakeet (*Psittacula krameri echo* (b) Carolina Parakeet (*Conuropsis carolinesis carolinensis* (c) Splendid Parakeet (*Neophema splendida* (d) Beautiful Parakeet (*Psephotus pulcherrimus*)

977. Which species of Parakeet nests in the nests of termite?
   (a) Mauritius Parakeet (*Psittacula krameri echo*)
   (b) Carolina Parakeet (*Conuropsis carolinesis*)
   (c) Splendid Parakeet (*Neophema splendida*)
   (d) Beautiful Parakeet (*Psephotus pulcherrimus*)

978. What is the Brolgas?
   (a) Crane (*Grus rubicundus*) (b) Tree (*Santalum album*) (c) Alligator (d) Extinct Parakeet

979. Name the only group of birds whose nostrils open at the tip of the bill:
   (a) Kiwis (b) Parrots (c) Parakeets (d) Owls

980. What is the Dragon's teeth (*Collocalia inexpecta¹a*) sold in China?
   (a) Nest of Edible Swiftlet (b) Eggs of the Parakeets (c) Bones of Ostrich (d) Feathers of sea birds.

981. Where are Kiwis (*Apteryx australis*) found?
   (a) New Zealand (b) South America (c) Africa (d) Australia

982. Where are Ostriches (*Struthio camelus*) found?
   (a) New Zealand (b) South America (c) Africa (d) Australia

983. Where are Emus (*Dromiceius novae-hollandae*) found?
   (a) New Zealand (b) South America (c) Africa (d) Australia

984. Where are Rheas (*Rhea americana*) found?
   (a) New Zealand (b) South America (c) Africa (d) Australia

985. How many species of birds in the world are known only from the fossils?
   (a) 900 (b) 1100 (c) 1300 (d) 1500

986. How many species of birds in the world have fossil as well as living representatives today?
(a) 800 (b) 1000 (c) 1200 (d) 1500

987. Massa National Park provides the breeding habitat for approximately half of the world's population of Waldrapp Ibis (*Geronticus eremita*). In which country is it located?
(a) Mexico (b) Bolivia (c) Australia (d) Morocco

988. Which of the following birds is extinct?
(a) Passenger Pigeon (*Ectopistes migratorius*)
(b) Mauritius Pink Pigeon (*Nesoenas mayeri*)
(c) Imperial Pigeon (*Ducula badia*) (d) Snow Pigeon (*Columba leuconota*)

989. Which bird was killed by natives of Venezuela to obtain the cooking oil?
(a) The Oil Bird (*Steatornis caripensis*)
(b) Passenger Pigeon (*Ectopistes migratorius*)
(c) Imperial Pigeon (*Ducula badia*) (d) Snow Pigeon (*Columba leuconota*)

990. Which is the most crop destructive bird in the world?
(a) Redbilled Quelea or Feathered Locust (*Quelea quelea*) (b) House Sparrow (*Passer domesiicus*) (c) Tree Sparrow (*Passer montanus*)
(d) None of the above

PHOTO QUIZ

991. Identify this deer photographed at Sariska National Park:
(a) Cheetal (*Axis axis*) (b) Hog Deer (*Axis porcinus*) (c) Sambhar (*Cervus unicolor*)

992. Identify this wild goat photographed at Eraviculum National Park:
(a) Chiru (*Pantholops hodgsoni*) (b) Takin (*Budorcas taxicolor*) (c) Nigiri Tahr (*Hemitragus hylocrius*)

993. Identify this Antelope photographed with Common Peafowl:
(a) Nilgai (*Boselaphus tragocamelus* (b) Chiru (*Pantholops hodgsoni*) (c) Takin (*Budorcas taxicolor*)

994. Identify this species of primate shown in the photograph:
(a) Liontailed Macaque (*Macaca silenus*) (b) Common Langur (*Presbytes entellus*) (c) Nilgiri Langur (*Presbytes johni*)

995. Identify the black-coloured bird sitting at the tip of the branch:
(a) House Crow (*Corvus splendens*) (b) Jungle Crow (*C. macrorhynchus*) (c) Little Cormorant (*Phalacrocorax niger*)

996. Identify the species of Stork depicted in the photograph:
(a) Openbilled Stork (*Anastomus oscitans*) (b) Adjutant (*Leptoptilos dubius*) (c) Painted Stork (*Mycteria leucocephala*)

997. Identify the Snake photographed with a green shrub:
(a) Common green snake (b) Green Python (c) Paradise Flying Snake

998. Identify this wild flowering tree photographed at Agora, Uttarkashi, in U.P.:
(a) Rhododendron (*Rhododendron arboreum*) (b) Red Ceder (*Toona australis*) (c) Red Wood (*Trochetiopsis erythroxylon*)

999. Name this palace on which a Tiger Reserve in India has been named:
(a) Periyar (b) Sariska (c) Dudhwa

1000. Identify this tree of myrobilon family showing reddish brown fruits:
(a) *Terminalia myriocarpa* (b) *Terminalia arjuna*
(c) *Terminalia chebula*

991

992

995

966

997

999

1000

ANSWERS

CHAPTER 1

1.a	2.a	3.b	4.c	5.b	6.a
7.c	8.d	9.d	10.b	11.b	12.b&c
are synonymous		13.a	14.c	15.a	16.d
17.b	18.b	19.a	20.a	21.b	22.c
23.a	24.c	25.a			

CHAPTER 2

26.a	27.a	28.d	29.a	30.a	31.a
32.d	33.a	34.a	35.b	36.a	37.c
38.b	39.c	40.a	41.d	42.d	43.c
44.b	45.c	46.a	47.b	48.a	49.c
50.b	51.a	52.a	53.d	54.b	55.a
56.b	57.d	58.d	59.a	60.b	61.c
62.a	63.a	64.c	65.a	66.c	67.c
68.c	69.a	70.a	71.d	72.d	73.a
74.d	75.a	76.c	77.c	78.b	79.b
80.a	81.b	82.d	83.c	84.c	85.a
86.c	87.c	88.c	89.a	90.a	91.b
92.d	93.d	94.b	95.a	96.a	97.a
98.a	99.d	100.a	101.a	102.c	103.c
104.b	105.a	106.a	107.d	108.a	109.b
110.b	111.a	112.d	113.a	114.a	115.a
116.b	117.a	118.b	119.a	120.a	121.a
122.b	123.b	124.b	125.b	126.a	127.b
128.d	129.a	130.d	131.d	132.b	133.c
134.c	135.c	136.a	137.d	138.a	139.a
140.c					

CHAPTER 3

141.d	142.d	143.d	144.a	145.d	146.a
147.c	148.b	149.b	150.c	151.c	152.c
153.a	154.a	155.a	156.a	157.d	158.c
159.a	160.c	161.a	162.c	163.a	164.b
165.b	166.d	167.a	168.c	169.a	170.b
171.d	172.a	173.a	174.b	175.c	176.b
177.a	178.a	179.a	180.a	181.d	182.d
183.a	184.d	185.a	186.b	187.a	188.a
189.a	190.c				

CHAPTER 4

191.c	192.b	193.b	194.a	195.a	196.d
197.c	198.a	199.c	200.a	201.b	202.d
203.a	204.a				

CHAPTER 5

205.a	206.b	207.b	208.a	209.c	210.d
211.a	212.a	213.b	214.a	215.a	216.a
217.a	218.a	219.b	220.c	221.c	222.a
223.c	224.b	225.a	226.b	227.a	228.a
229.a	230.a	231.b	232.a	233.a	234.b
235.a	236.b	237.a	238.a	239.a	240.a
241.c	242.a	243.a	244.a	245.b	246.a
247.b	248.d	249.b	250.a	251.a	252.b
253.c	254.a	255.c	256.a	257.a	258.b
259.c					

CHAPTER 6

260.d	261.a	262.a	263.a	264.a	265.a
266.b	267.b	268.a	269.b	270.a	271.b
272.a	273.a	274.a	275.a	276.a	277.a
278.c	279.d	280.a	281.a	282.a	283.d
284.d	285.a	286.c	287.a	288.c	289.a

290.c	291.b	292.a	293.d	294.a	295.a
296.a	297.d	298.a	299.b	300.a	301.d
302.a	303.d	304.a	305.a	306.a	307.a
308.a	309.a	310.a	311.a	312.a	313.a
314.a	315.a	316.c	317.b	318.a	319.d
320.a	321.a	322.a	323.a	324.a	325.a
326.a	327.a	328.a	329.a	330.b	331.a
332.a	333.a	334.a	335.b	336.a	337.a
338.a	339.a	340.a	341.a	342.a	343.a
344.a	345.a	346.a	347.b	348.a	349.a
350.a	351.a	352.a	353.d	354.a	355.a
356.b	357.c	358.c	359.a	360.a	361.a
362.a	363.a	364.b	365.a	366.b	367.a
368.a	369.a	370.a	371.a	372.a	373.a
374.b	375.a	376.a	377.a	378.b	379.a
380.b	381.a	382.a	383.a	384.a	385.a
386.b	387.b	388.a	389.a	390.c	391.b
392.a	393.a	394.b	395.a	396.a	397.a
398.a	399.a	400.a	401.a	402.c	403.c
404.b	405.a	406.b	407.b	408.b	409.a
410.b	411.a	412.a	413.c	414.b	415.a
416.a	417.a	418.a	419.a	420.a	421.a
422.a	423.a	424.b	425.c	426.a	427.b
428.a	429.b	430.a	431.a	432.a	433.a
434.a	435.a	436.c	437.c	438.a	439.a
440.b	441.a	442.a	443.a	444.b	445.a
446.a	447.b	448.a	449.a	450.a	451.c
452.a	453.c	454.b	455.a	456.d	457.c
458.a	459.b	460.a	461.a	462.b	463.a
464.a	465.b	466.a	467.a	468.b	469.a
470	471.a	472.a	473.a	474.a	475.a
476.a	477.a	478.a	479.a	480.a	481.a
482.c	483.a	484.b	485.a	486.a	487.a
488.a	489.a	490.a	491.a	492.b	493.d
494.d	495.a	496.a	497.a	498.b	499.a
500.a	501.a	502.d	503.b	504.b	505.a

506.a	507.b	508.a	509.a	510.c	511.d
512.a	513.b	514.a	515.d	516.b	517.a
518.b	519.a	520.a	521.b	522.a	523.b
524.a	525.a	526.b	527.b	528.a	529.a
530.d	531.a	532.a	533.a		

CHAPTER 7

534.a	535.c	536.a	537.a	538.b	539.a
540.a	541.a	542.c	543.b	544.a	545.a
546.a	547.a	548.b	549.a	550.a	551.a
552.d	553.a	554.c	555.b	556.a	557.a
558.a	559.b	560.a	561.a	562.a	563.c
564.d	565.a	566.b	567.b	568.c	569.b
570.c	571.d	572.b	573.a	574.a	575.d
576.a	577.a	578.c	579.a	580.a	581.d
582.a	583.a	584.b	585.a	586.a	587.b
588.b	589.a	590.a	591.a	592.b	593.a
594.a	595.b	596.a	597.a	598.b	599.b
600.b	601.c	602.a	603.a	604.a	605.b
606.a	607.a	608.c	609.a	610.a	611.a
612.a	613.c	614.a	615.a	616.a	617.a
618.a	619.a	620.d	621.b	622.a	623.a
624.b	625.b	626.a	627.b	628.a	629.d
630.a	631.c	632.d	633.a	634.b	635.a
636.a	637.b	638.a	639.a	640.a	641.a
642.a	643.a	644.a	645.d	646.b	647.a
648.a	649.c	650.a	651.a	652.c	653.a
654.a	655.a	656.a	657.d	658.a	659.b
660.b	661.b	662.a	663.a	664.a	665.a
666.a	667.a	668.b	669.b	670.a	671.a
672.a	673.a	674.b	675.a	676.a	677.c
678.a	679.a	680.b	681.a	682.d	683.d
684.c	685.d	686.a	687.c	688.c	689.c
690.a	691.a	692.d	693.a	694.a	695.a
696.a	697.b	698.a	699.b	700.a	701.a

| 702.a | 703.a | 704.a | 705.c | 706.c | 707.c |
| 708.d | 709.a | 710.a | | | |

CHAPTER 8

711.a	712.c	713.a	714.c	715.b	716.a
717.b	718.a	719.a	720.c	721.b	722.a
723.a	724.a	725.a	726.a	727.a	728.d
729.a	730.d	731.d	732.a	733.d	734.b
735.a	736.a	737.a	738.a	739.d	740.d
741.d	742.b	743.a	744.a	745.c	746.a
747.a	748.a	749.a	750.a	751.a	752.c
753.a	754.a	755.a	756.a	757.c	758.b
759.a	760.a	761.a	762.d	763.c	764.b
765.c	766.a	767.c	768.a	769.c	770.a
771.a	772.a	773.a	774.a	775.a	776.a
777.a	778.a	779.a	780.d	781.a	782.a
783.a	784.b	785.a	786.a	787.b	788.d
789.a	790.a	791.a	792.d	793.d	794.a
795.b	796.b	797.b	798.c	799.c	800.a
801.a	802.a	803.a	804.a	805.d	806.c
807.c	808.d	809.a	810.a	811.a	812.a

CHAPTER 9

813.d	814.a	815.a	816.a	817.c	818.a
819.a	820.c	821.a	822.a	823.b	824.a
825.a	826.c				

CHAPTER 10

827.a	828.b	829.c	830.b	831.a	832.a
833.b	834.b	835.d	836.a	837.a	838.c
839.a	840.a	841.a			

CHAPTER 11

842.a	843.b	844.b	845.a	846.a	847.b
848.d	849.c	850.b	851.a	852.a	853.b
854.a	855.a	856.c	857.a	858.a	859.c
860.a	861.a	862.d	863.a	864.c	865.a
866.b	867.a	868.c	869.c	870.a	871.c
872.a	873.a	874.a	875.d	876.a	877.a
878.a	879.a	880.a	881.a	882.b	883.d
884.a	885.d	886.a	887.c	888.d	889.a
890.d	891.a	892.c	893.a	894.a	895.a

CHAPTER 12

896.a	897.c	898.d	899.a	900.a	901.a
902.a	903.a	904.d	905.a	906.e	907.c
908.a	909.a	910.a	911.a	912.a	913.a
914.a	915.d	916.a	917.a	918.a	919.a
920.d	921.a	922.a	923.b	924.a	925.a
926.a	927.b	928.a	929.a	930.a	931.a
932.d	933.c	934.b	935.a	936.d	937.a
938.b	939.c	940.b	941.a	942.a	943.b
944.a	945.a	946.a	947.a	948.a	949.a
950.a	951.b	952.a	953.a	954.a	955.b
956.a	957.a	958.a	959.a	960.a	961.a
962.b	963.a	964.a	965.a	966.c	967.b
968.a	969.a	970.d	971.a	972.a	973.a
974.a	975.a	976.b	977.d	978.a	979.a
980.a	981.a	982.c	983.d	984.b	985.a
986.a	987.d	988.a	989.a	990.a	

PHOTO QUIZ

991.c	992.c	993.a	994.c	995.c	996.c
997.a	998.a	999.b	1000.a		

www.ingramcontent.com/pod-product-compliance
Lightning Source LLC
Chambersburg PA
CBHW050347030726
47503CB00008B/2663